DATE DUE	
SEP 13 2010		
AUG 1 9 2012		

Praise for Mark Swartz's *Instant Karma*:

"Welcome to the oddball world of David Felsenstein, a Chicago loner who's part Young Werther, part Travis Bickle and part post-adolescent Borges . . . a kind of Dewey Decimal tribute to Paul Auster's *Leviathan.*"—*Los Angeles Times*

"A contemporary and even tender *Diary of a Madman.*"—*The Believer*

"[a] concentrated and diabolically clever novel . . . a tricky puzzle of a tale."—*Chicago Tribune*

"Insta-good, a tour de force, an engaging, farcical, joyful reprise of 1000 great ideas tumbling around in one humble brain, in one ordinary body."—Frederick Barthelme

"*Instant Karma* is clever and well written; in a sense, Felsenstein reminds us of Dostoevsky's antihero in *Notes from Underground*, with spectacular violence being the metaphor here for the alienation of modern life."—*Library Journal*

"[An] intriguing debut."—*Publishers Weekly*

"A new and prodigious talent."—Harry Mathews

" . . . a first novel of remarkable compression, lithe satirical humor, impressive intellectual dimension, and sly provocation..."—*Booklist*

"Imagine a collaboration between David Sedaris and David Foster Wallace on a book about the interrelationship of art and anarchy"
—*Washington City Paper*

"Funny, erudite, tender, and sad, *Instant Karma* traces the mental disintegration of a young man's journey from solitary bilbiophile to Dada-library terrorist. But the book is also a meditation on our fragmented culture—that mysterious hodge-podge of conflicting images and myriad bits of text that threaten to destroy all possible meaning. In Mark Swartz's hapless anti-hero, David Felsenstein, the distance between incendiary idea and literal explosion becomes both dangerously small and frighteningly real."—Siri Hustvedt

"In a first novel of remarkable compression, lithe satirical humor, impressive intellectual dimension, and sly provocation, Swartz creates a lost soul who is both endearing and alarming, and raises difficult questions about freedom and isolation, knowledge and fanaticism, creativity and nihilism."—*Booklist*

"Imagine a collaboration between David Sedaris and David Foster Wallace on a book about the interrelationship of art and anarchy. . . . What you end up with is Mark Swartz's weird but wonderful *Instant Karma*."—*Washington City Paper*

"An obsessive read about an obsessive reader, Mark Swartz's *Instant Karma* is a book with the sort of power that makes you remember the sort of power books have."—Daniel Handler

"What a pleasure it is to read a book that is so wholly itself—contained and furious, timely and profound, and deeply, rigorously smart. I underlined passage after passage, as Swartz synthesizes the voices of countless other authors with his own, making a book built of books, creating both castles and rubble in the reader's mind. A striking debut."—Aimee Bender, author of *The Girl in the Flammable Skirt*

H O A N E

:

2 B Y

$M_{ARK\ SWARTZ}$ }

O

V

L

To Jennie

"The Lord said to Moses, 'Take the staff, and you and your brother Aaron gather the assembly together. Speak to that rock before their eyes and it will pour out its water. You will bring water out of the rock for the community so they and their livestock can drink.' So Moses took the staff from the Lord's presence, just as he commanded him. He and Aaron gathered the assembly together in front of the rock and Moses said to them, 'Listen, you rebels, must we bring you water out of this rock?' Then Moses raised his arm and struck the rock twice with his staff. Water gushed out, and the community and their livestock drank."

—Numbers 20: 7–11

"Water is the last infrastructure frontier for private investors."

—Johan Bastin, European Bank for
Reconstruction and Development, 1999

11-06
19⁰⁰ pnb

H$_2$O
© Mark Swartz

ISBN: 1-933368-19-5
ISBN-13: 978-1933-36819-1

Published by Soft Skull Press
55 Washington St., Suite 804
Brooklyn, NY 11201
www.softskull.com

Distributed by Publishers Group West
www.pgw.com 1-800-788-3123

Design: Gary Fogelson
Cover type illustrations: Phil Lubliner
Back cover photo: Larry Lubliner

Printed in Canada

An excerpt of this novel appeared in the summer 2005 issue of
BOMB.

Library of Congress Cataloging-in-Publication data available
from the Library of Congress.

Thank you: Andrew Blauner, Michael Cohen, Scott Cohen, Dave Davies, Ammi Emergency, Adam Freyer, Luke Gerwe, Jennie Guilfoyle, Laurie Guilfoyle, David Hart, Joan Harvey, Jane Jiambalvo, Burns Magruder, Marcie Muscat, Richard Nash, Jim Poniewozik, Amy Jean Porter, Kristin Pulkkinen, Dan Ramsden, Rob Rush, Steve Simon, Betsy Sussler, Laurel Swartz, Michael Swartz, Robert Swartz

CHAPTER ONE

As the sun slid behind a huddle of naked towers, the hotel's photo-sensitive curtain-wall system responded with a well-stocked bar of color transformations: from stout to port, from cabernet to scotch whisky, from gold rum to champagne, then the color of just-poured seltzer. The temperature dropped below freezing without dispersing the static electricity that Chicago accumulates in winter.

At the front desk I tried to charm my way into a room upgrade, but the plastic-complexioned woman withdrew behind a chilled smile.

"Name?"

"Shivers."

Unfortunately, she said, the Executive Suites were all booked, but would I like her to put me down for a table in the Pepper Mill? After this evening, reservations would be hard to come by. She looked like she'd be cool to the touch: even the hair was frosted. When I asked what was good in the restaurant, she laughed courteously and started to turn away, but then, asking my name again, remembered there was a message for me. Would I wait there just a minute?

The Brahms lobby smelled like spent fireworks. Plumes of smoke rose up through the light fixtures toward the distant glassy heights of the atrium, where slanted gills failed to stir the air.

The way the smoke softened the light made everybody look slightly debauched. Young executives were swinging hand-tooled leather bags and fetching each other frothy cocktails. I noticed high-end sport coats and Italian shoes, rows of even white teeth set in glowing bronze faces, bodies engineered like aerodynamic instruments. A silk banner billowed from the top of the atrium: Zodia Welcomes the Northeast Tax Action.

I took a seat at the bar, alternately chewing cashews and lighting them on fire. Beside me two Zodiacs conversed, a prelude to something sordid.

"I heard," said one, "the architect was a blind man from Brazil."

"Argentina, actually," said the other. (She was the type who used the word actually quite often.) "Desvio-Jardin."

"I could die here in this lobby. Happily."

"This atrium. Legally blind, but his buildings are works of art. An engineering feat without precedent, anchoring the building into the riverbed. The current supplies half the hotel's electricity and maintains a steady temperature in the rooms summer and winter."

"You wouldn't believe the water pressure in my room. It's like being massaged by bullets."

"The Brahms is also a destination for a special kind of pilgrimage, each spring. Every year around this time, the sick and the blind register at the hotel and order a predawn wakeup call. When the hour comes, they take the elevator down to the lobby and, on their own or perhaps with some assistance, drag their seats to the atrium. The first half hour or forty minutes of daylight have a particular quality."

"Something quite spiritual."

"It's incredibly physical, actually."

"Yes, I think I'm feeling it. Or maybe that's the vodka lemon!"

"And the thing about it is. The thing is that this architectural effect, if that's what you call it, cannot be reproduced. Other architects have attempted to remake the building in different cities, using the same designs, the same materials."

"Nothing."

"Yes, some things happen only once."

All nuts burn, but some kinds burn better than others. The cashews burnt blue and very slowly, leaving smudges and piles of ash in a foil ashtray. The viability of nuts as an alternative energy source was occupying my mind when the desk attendant beckoned with a small square card.

Miyumi Park, Human Resources

Same logo as mine—a crystal trident—same raised lettering, same card stock, and yet an unfamiliar sensation shot up my arm to my heart. I knew myself to be capable of falling painfully in love with a dimple in the street or a well-turned ankle on a staircase, but this was my first time with a business card.

Partly it was the name, of course, that me-you-me promise of complex mattress gymnastics, but much deadlier was the moist oval, still warm, from the bearer's thumb pad. You could almost make out the whorls, and they didn't belong to the chilly hand on the other side of the desk.

I reclaimed my barstool and requested a lemonade. Sometimes it doesn't help to have advance notice before making a first impression, and when she approached I was in the process of attempting not to rehearse what to say first. Her hair swayed, her skin glowed. Her waist joined her hips obscenely beneath all that wool. Her eyes never stopped monitoring the lobby. She asked what I was drinking.

"Assuming the glass holds eight ounces," I responded, "that would be seven ounces water, the rest comprising sodium fluoride, sodium hydroxide, potassium permanganate . . . " After another sip, I added, "phenylalanine, aspartic acid, and petroleum-based lemon flavoring. Plus other trace elements too numerous to mention. Would you like one?"

There were three big public-private ventures in town. Zodia brought newspapers, garbage collection, and law enforcement under one umbrella, and the former think tank that still went by

3

the name Committee of Lifelong Access oversaw universities, real estate, and beverages other than water. Drixa did water, utilities, and the post.

With the scarf at her throat, cameo on her collar, gold bracelet on one perfumed wrist, analog watch on the other, Miyumi had the air of a more graceful time, though her outlook was thoroughly contemporary. She emphasized Drixa's policy of fielding an extremely wide range of candidates for top positions. The appointment of a Chief Engineer would help to chart the company's course for the next several years, and she had the freedom to interview anybody she had even the slightest hunch about, regardless of background and experience. "That's why I'm with Drixa," she said, "because they let me experiment. Science made this company great, so why should experimentation stop at the lab?"

"I do like the idea," I said, not certain whether I was being told that I was a candidate for Chief Engineer. "Of running everything like an experiment. Once you set up the conditions, you stick with them and wait to see how things turn out. If you altered them in the middle, you'd never know whether your outcome resulted from the first conditions, the second conditions, or from the switch. Experiments are to learn from." This was a lie. Scientists altered their experiments midstream all the time. Knowing how to fudge data was what separated the good ones from the bad ones. But even I knew better than to tell the truth about the truth during what might be a job interview.

"Exactly," Miyumi said, squeezing my kneecap encouragingly. Her long, elegant hand weighed hardly anything, and the warmth through my pants multiplied in my bloodstream. "As you know, we've run a few experiments of our own this past year, and we've always had Lionel's total support, even when things got crazy with the four-day workweek."

"It was my understanding that the staff overwhelmingly preferred that system. Many of us considered it, if not an outright success, then a valuable experience for the entire company. It's a nice hotel."

"We never said not to go home; we just provided the hotel rooms for Monday, Tuesday, and Wednesday if you wanted to stay. A lot of people took advantage of our offer, and most of those people thought it worked. I thought it worked. Sure, there were some complications, and we hadn't anticipated the way the *Tribune* would go after us, but personally? Personally I got to know people in ways that wouldn't have been possible under traditional workplace routines. Those relationships I built during those six weeks are already proving valuable going forward."

"If people get bent out of shape, hallelujah. Who says things can't snap back into shape after you're done stretching them?"

"Egg-ZACT-ly!" Miyumi said. "Who says? And what good is a company where people aren't willing to be wrong once in while? That's how Lionel puts it. If you bet right every time, you're betting too safe."

As with the leaders of all successful companies, Drixa's was invariably referred to by his first name. I knew him only from video but felt a special kinship with him because he, too, had once designed filters.

As Assistant Designer, Filters and Drains, I had never thought of myself as Chief Engineer material. I had the engineering degree from Cal Tech and the Brooks Brothers suit (second-hand, anyway), but the qualities and imponderables that distinguished a leader were nevertheless missing from my posture, which never seemed to find a comfortable notch between slouching and standing at attention; and my gaze, which consistently landed on the far sides of intensity and slackness. Not to mention my handshake, which always seemed to grip too early or too late.

She said, "Tell me about your strengths and weaknesses. Don't skimp on the weaknesses, either. I've heard them all."

"I worry too much about the wrong things and not enough about the right things. I remember all kinds of things better forgotten and vice versa. And . . . " Then I remembered how to act during a job interview, if that's what this was. "Strength one, creative. Strength two, focused. Three, *total dedication to the Drixa mission.*" My impression of Drixa Director Lionel Dawson's feathery rumble required no explanation.

"Don't forget snappy dresser." She twiddled a cufflink.

"That's a custom-made twill shirt."

"Custom made for somebody, anyhow," she allowed. Plucking a tiny phone from her bag, Miyumi paused to let the winterlight play a melody on her lips. "Okay, here's your big chance," she said.

"You're Lionel, and the car you sent for your dinner companions is late. Tell them it's not acceptable."

Like much of the staff, I had an impersonation of Lionel Dawson, but mine was recognized as uncanny. I let some gravel into my larynx: "This is Lionel. The car I sent . . . Yes, no, it's still not there. This is unacceptable." I asked rhetorically, "How long have they been waiting there? Upwards of twenty minutes?"

"Upwards," she confirmed.

"Upwards," I repeated and hit the off button.

"Onwards," she said, slipping the phone into my inside jacket pocket. She took my arm and walked me to the car at the moment it rolled into the breezeway. We climbed on all fours into the back, giggling like prom dates.

"Ooh, tinted."

"That's not your buckle, Hayden, it's mine."

"Wait, but. Oh, yeah, sorry."

Sensing my befuddlement, Miyumi said, "Just wait, you'll be right where you belong. An Executive Suite with Jacuzzi, fireplace, fluffy robes, and a lake view." She parted her lips with the confidence of someone who had spent long years listening and could now speak effectively and appropriately: "In 1899 they changed the direction of the Chicago River. Isn't it astonishing? Think about that next time you're struggling to part your hair straight."

I smiled back, wondering if I'd been mistaken for somebody else. Yet I hadn't done anything to give a false impression. True, I hadn't said, "I'm not who you think I am. I'm just staying at the hotel while my wife, my estranged wife, packs my belongings." But she hadn't asked.

If confronted, I was ready to assert that I thought she was somebody else.

"How do you change the direction of a river?" Miyumi asked. It was known that high-level job interviews involved tests of the candidate's creative reasoning.

"First you dam it up, I suppose, and then you alter the inclination of the riverbed. Then you sort of teach the water to flow backwards, and gradually it gets accustomed to the new direction. They'll be in trouble if they ever have to change it back, though."

She seemed to think that what I said was cute. I wished I'd shaved a second time. "I actually have a few questions for you," I said, remembering another maneuver expected in a job interview.

"Not so fast!" she replied, on the brink of a giggle. "It's all happening so fast, isn't it?"

"In a way."

"It is pretty funny when you think about it," she said, checking the time on her watch—without, however, permitting me a glimpse—before resting a hand on my knee. "But at least we're keeping our sense of humor."

Our car crawled past the controversial new waterworks, "celebrating the historic partnership of the City of Chicago and the Drixa Corporation." Over an unnerving, ruthless noise from within the gargantuan brick edifice, our driver honked encouragingly to the knot of seven or eight protestors gathered out front. Some of them mistook the honk for criticism and looked angry. It's quite difficult to show encouragement with a honk.

Miyumi told the driver to cross the river, and soon we skirted a particularly elegant lattice system for rainwater and sewage evacuation, and I felt myself nodding with approval; they were my pipes.

"Some people out there seem to have a slight problem with Drixa," I observed.

"ICE-9. Whoever heard of environmentalists protesting clean

water? I mean, if they want to drink the poison falling down from the sky, more power to them, but don't tell me to boycott the service we provide and then tell me it's to save the environment."

"Still, give them credit for caring."

"Well, of course," she said. "But they're completely missing the point. I've been with Drixa for nine years, and we've reinvented ourselves five times in response to changing realities, overnight, never forgetting our core mission. You can bet there were plenty of lawsuits."

"Well, *lawsuits*," I said the word like it was a childish concern. Lawsuits. Cooties.

"Exactly," she confirmed. "Lionel is more than a visionary; he's a visionary with teeth."

"Everyone's excited about the new plant," I ventured. "Safer, cleaner, more efficient."

"It's okay Hayden, he's with us."

I compared the photo on the taxi license to what I could see of the driver's face and was satisfied it was the same man. Pierre Amu Lucluc, a burly uncle with a wide, dark-pink face and a black mustache. Was it the driver himself, or his company, who had ordered the sign posted on the back of the driver's seat?

HOW'M I DRIVING? DO I SOMETIMES FORGET TO SIGNAL BEFORE CHANGING LANES? DO I BRAKE TOO ABRUPTLY OR GIVE HER TOO MUCH GAS WHEN THE LIGHT TURNS GREEN? CAN YOU HEAR ME MUTTERING AT THE OTHER CARS? WHAT GOES THROUGH MY MIND AS I START THIS VEHICLE IN THE MORNING BEFORE A FULL DAY OF BATTLING AN OBSOLETE TRAFFIC PLAN? WHAT WAS LIFE LIKE FOR ME BEFORE I TOOK THIS JOB? WHAT KIND OF PERSON AM I, DEEP DOWN? P.A.LUCLUC 312-2222-LIMO

To Lucluc's credit, the inside of the cab was clean and well ventilated, circulating just the faintest amount of Miyumi's nervous musk past my nostrils. Her nervousness helped me to relax. There was plenty of legroom, and I liked the way the seatback supported my backbone.

"Of course he is."

The closer we got to the restaurant, the heavier the silences between us weighed. Each of us put on like the other was a Drixa favorite and we ourselves replaceable.

"Human Resources must be sizzling these days, with all the growth the company has seen."

"Engineering, that's where the sizzle is. Without innovation, it's all just plumbing."

Looking back toward the slowly receding waterworks, I said,

"Maybe, but you hire the plumbers."

"Come on, Hayden, we wouldn't be here if you weren't some kind of genius."

"Why are we here, Miyumi?"

"No idea!" More laughter.

"But really, I'm not brilliant as a scientist, nor do I have the stamina required of the workhorse, but I do have my tricks. My antennae, very occasionally, pick up a genius signal, and the trick is tuning in."

What would the driver know that I wouldn't? Was the plant a fake? Nobody had told me. As project assistant, I wasn't in on the overall plans for the overhaul of the filtration system but like everyone else had followed the debate surrounding its construction. Like a virus mutating to outsmart a vaccine, pollutants had repeatedly recombined to defeat each successive generation of filter technologies. One public health crisis followed another in devastating succession, with Drixa somehow emerging as the savior each time, rather than the culprit, though that would have been a fair description, too.

The newest purification facility supposedly represented a

quantum leap, the only drawback being a terrible rumble that could be heard for miles despite the best acoustic controls. An exemption to noise pollution laws had quickly been ratified over familiar protests from the Independent Council for the Environment, who trotted out psychologists warning of deep city-wide distraction that would result from an enveloping hum. Fear propels radical decisions. Now it seemed that the awesome sound amounted to nothing more than a marketing ploy. It was an old trick: in product demonstrations, customers invariably select the louder of two vacuum cleaners of equal power.

As we inched through an agony of traffic, I found myself savoring my own ignorance, the pleasure of rolling through unexplained circumstance. It pains me now to remember that peculiar pleasure, like the memory of a gorgeous bird approaching before the realization dawns that it's a bird of prey. But this was before I set eyes on Aqua Bella. And this was before I discovered the means to grab controlling interest in one of the world's great companies and the luck of fumbling it before I could score. And this was before the spectacle of a drowned world went fom possibility to probability.

Chapter Two

All the drivers circling Giorgio & Gina's to avoid parking lot charges just exacerbated the traffic. The lot was empty. Inside bustled with an expense-account and taxpayer's-dime crowd. We approached a gray-templed man at an alcove table.

In recent months, I'd plunged through strata of admiration and suspicion, reverence and contempt, worship and hostility, down to a molten core of mingled love and hate redolent of what assassins must feel toward their victims. Along the way I'd assembled an extensive library and archive of Lionel Dawson's career, complete with video files for perfecting the impersonation. His vocal mannerisms and repertory of gestures became second nature as I set foot on the path of *inventrepreneurship*, a word whose coinage he necessitated. I could duplicate his signature. His worldview was etched inside my eyelids. Hell, it's not like I ever had one of my own to preserve.

And here I was, his guest for dinner, and I doubted my ability to manage knife and fork, let alone intelligent conversation. Miyumi complimented his black-on-charcoal necktie. From there, she moved onto his suit and pocket square. Lionel and I wore nearly identical black suits, but where the material of his jacket whispered grace and control, mine bunched up on my torso like a lawn bag stuffed with wet clippings. His face was smooth; you could strike a match on mine.

There was a suede bag, superbly aged, at his feet. This was a man who always ate with his back to the wall. His manner was

Hollywood-corrupt-lieutenant: gallant, even dandyish, but with an undertone of weariness. It said, *With the shit I'm given to work with, all I can pray for is something other than total disaster. If you pull anything flashy, you're dead. If you screw up, even with the best intentions, you're dead.* A pair of lifetime waiters showed him genuine affection. His presence assured them they worked in a classy establishment.

"And your hair, it's different, isn't—"

"Thank you, Miyumi." Lionel sipped his Country Life Lemonade. "We don't want to waste any time. I'm sure we all have places we'd rather be right now. The sooner we clarify matters here, the sooner we can be on our way to those places."

"We need menus," I said.

Lionel smirked, "I've taken the liberty of ordering." He looked like someone who had served as president of his high school class but soon discovered that governments don't work. His eyes were dark and unbelieving, like his tie. At his signal, our three glasses were ceremoniously filled with icewater. The group at the next table noticed this extravagance and decided to order a bottle for themselves.

"I hear that everything's good here," I said, "especially the ice cream."

"Special cows," Miyumi agreed. It was common knowledge about Giorgio & Gina's. Obscene attentions were lavished on the dairy livestock.

To start with, I was hoping for red meat, something to bite down on. It was still registering with me that I was sitting with Lionel Dawson, the man who made water what it was today. My ambition was to make it what it would be tomorrow, but so far my experiments had proved inconclusive at best.

Miyumi explained that I was very grateful for the opportunity. When Lionel made a sarcastic sound that was a combination of *he ought to be grateful* and *he doesn't look grateful enough*, she made a kissy face, like she would at a vicious puppy on the other side of a chain link fence.

"I was just telling Hayden how much Drixa appreciates his dedication. Especially these days."

"The reason I'm here is to say I'll do whatever I can to help. The work you've done so far has been terrific," Lionel began. "Your contributions have gone, what can I say but, above and beyond."

"I don't see what the big deal is," I answered. "There's nothing I could point to yet and say, 'That's something I'm proud of.'"

"That's very modest of you."

"Besides my son, of course."

"That I can understand. My daughter—"

"His daughter," Miyumi chimed in.

"I've learned a lot from her, or rather, having a daughter has taught me."

Normally, they say not to dwell on family during interviews, but here was something like an invitation. "Hayden Jr. is like a crystal ball," I said. "It doesn't happen every time, and of course it doesn't happen right away, but being with him . . . I find myself realizing things that wouldn't otherwise have come forward, and in an instant I know them so well I don't even have to write them down."

Lionel grinned. "You've gone above and beyond. You've indicated a willingness to go *above and beyond* above and beyond."

"Thank you."

"And all the way to Malta."

Uh oh. "I think you're giving me too much credit."

Lionel made meaningful eye contact. "When somebody at Drixa goes above and beyond, Drixa responds with an equal and opposite force. We have a Letter of Agreement for you to sign."

"Letter?"

"I think you'll find all the standard language."

"That sounds reasonable to me, but like I said, the whole drains and filters team has—"

"Take your time. Show it to your lawyer. You'll come around." A sealed standard envelope sliced the air, and I didn't hesitate before sticking it under my seat.

"Let's give him the benefit of the doubt," Miyumi said. "See how intimidated he is?"

"Who's intimidating him?"

"Who. Vintage icewater with the director. 'I've taken the liberty.' Ever notice the effect that has?" She rattled her ice cubes at him.

Lionel turned to me. "Do I intimidate you?" He looked like he wanted the answer to be no, so I said yes, to prove I wasn't intimidated. There was laughter, but it increased tension rather than dissolving it. The waiter set a plate down in front of me, a large salad loaded with anchovies, pickled beets, and bits of egg that made me shudder.

"Something wrong?"

"No, it's just that, eggs and I, not simpatico." With a tilt of the director's head, the plate vanished.

"Maybe it all started in the summer of 1985," I elaborated. "With a mouthful of eggwater at the drinking fountain. Even after learning that sulfur was the cause, I had lost my taste for eggs. And nearly for water too. The taste coated my tongue for days, and all of the subsequent liquids I tried nauseated me except for something called bug juice, containing, I was promised, no bugs." I looked up to see that the story was not winning me any points. "But this water," I continued. "It's really good."

"Reminds me of when we were kids," Miyumi said.

"No, I mean it's really good."

"Growing up, we had this green cup on our bathroom counter," she recalled. "Nobody ever washed it, and nobody ever used it, either. The plastic was encrusted with the dried spray of a million toothbrush strokes. My brothers and I just stuck our heads under the faucet and lapped the water with our tongues. That was some good water."

Lionel said, "Organizations have replaced God, Shivers. Ignore them at your peril, but try too hard to comprehend them, and the miracle of their existence blows to smithereens. Faith works best at a respectful distance, and you have to guard against becoming too evangelical." He turned to acknowledge Miyumi's nodding head. "But also against being too atheistic."

"He knows that," she said.

"I do," I assured him. A version of this speech had been given the year before at a dinner honoring Dawson's lifetime contribution to science. He'd led into the religious comparison by way of an exhortation to forget previous orthodoxies, "to forget, indeed, everything thought to be sacred." The relatively tame outcry from various religious groups had quickly faded.

"This is very encouraging," Lionel continued. "And very gratifying to me personally. Now it's simply a matter of preparation, of communication, of execution. I feel one hundred percent confidence in both of you." I could see the man's contempt for Miyumi and mistrusted the compliment.

"Preparation, communication, execution," she repeated.

"Are we going to have dessert?" I asked. Miyumi announced that the driver was waiting, but I couldn't help adding, "Maybe just a scoop."

"Miyumi, for Christ's sake, let the man have some dessert!" We all laughed and sighed. A fruit plate appeared at the center of the table, consisting mainly of green grapes the size of fists.

"One more thing," Dawson said as he rose from the table. "The *Tribune* will take an interest. Check with Miyumi before you talk to them. Miyumi, check with me."

If the handshake that concluded the meal was a five-second baseball game, my team would have been shut out, my performance a Cubs-caliber catalogue of errors, failed stratagems, and tentative, lackluster motions. At one point I had to dry my palm on my lapel.

Miyumi must have caught a ride with the victor. I was too impressed to manage embarrassment. The meeting must have had its intended effect, because as I made my way on foot, the entire city seemed to take after the director. Making do with what it was given. The face it showed the world was the face it showed itself, but that didn't make it true, just consistent. The whiff of a tremendously overburdened infrastructure remained in the air notwithstanding the many cosmetic programs that had been instituted. Despite the population quintupling, it was no longer the capital of industry as in days past. Its mayoral dynasty had exceeded the point of diminishing returns: electoral challenges were weak because the prize had lost its sparkle, now that all of the major governmental functions were outsourced.

And me, I was the drain guy, a glorified plumber. Still, it was suddenly clear to me—and I credit Dawson for bringing forth the insight—that many problems in this world came down to plumbing. Traffic jams resulted from poor accounting for flow of vehicles. Economic downturns resulted from mismanagement of the flow of wealth through society. Most medical problems could be traced to blockages, bursts, and slow leaks. Human relations on the micro and macro scales—analyzed in vain by psychologists, game theorists, and political scientists—were best understood in the vocabulary of plumbing: flush out waste material. Filter out impurities. Build in valves to relieve pressure. Expunge the sticky and the disruptive, with force if necessary. And clean up thoroughly when you're done.

CHAPTER THREE

Thanks to adjacency to a large body of unspoiled freshwater, Chicago had come out at the end of the Water Crisis of '07–13 in comparably decent shape, except for the traffic. Multitudes migrating from the coasts had crammed the streets with fuel-efficient cars licensed in the dry zones of the southwest, the northeast, and the southeast and swelled the city to a city-state stretching from Cedar Rapids to Toledo, from St. Paul to Louisville. Native Chicagoans, granted economic and legal privileges, strolled the avenues in full confidence of their fine accomplishment. Business proposals involving land use and utilities could not win proper certification without third-generation Chicagoans on board. This ordinance led to awkward hierarchies, with lesser citizens serving as clandestine executives at considerably lower salaries than the three-piece-suited figureheads with their names on the doors of operations ranging from professional sports and overseas shipping to transportation and waste-removal systems.

Considering that my wife came from a well-known Chicago family, you might think I'd have little to complain about. The marriage, however, was doomed, and that was why I headed west on Grand Avenue with heavy shoes.

The Justice Complex occupied four city blocks, with a courtyard in the middle, empty besides two shabbily sculpted shrubs and a youngish security guard too busy arguing with his phone to notice me. "You're Julian Dameron's lawyer?" said the woman from behind bulletproof glass. She made a toy-motorcycle sound with the labyrinthine neon drinking straw that grew from her lemonade can.

"No, he's *my* lawyer. My name is Hayden Shivers." Everything about this arrangement was awkward. Impatient to begin the proceedings, Ginelle had asked her lawyer to refer me to one, and I stupidly calculated that appeasement would lead to reconciliation.

The receptionist spoke into a wall-mounted intercom: "Julian Dameron's lawyer is here." I resisted the urge to correct her. The drinking straw pointed to a sloppily painted red steel door a few feet away. Inside, the light was gentler. Julian stood there—or rather, he leaned, which was his customary attitude—dressed in a three-piece pinstripe suit coordinated to match the tapestries on the wall, the well-stocked bookshelves and wet bar.

I lowered myself into an overstuffed 1980s chair, not sure how to begin, wondering if this was a form of incarceration, despite the manor house décor. Julian cut an imposing, ducal figure, even though he was somewhat ice cream cone shaped. There was a painting in a gilt frame, perhaps a portrait of one of Julian's ancestors. The sitter had a smile-concealing salt-and-pepper mustache and the gravity of a formerly great football or rugby player. A survivor of serious knee injuries.

"You look okay," he said, not looking at me. "Considering."

"I checked into the Brahms," I replied. "They take care of you there."

"View?"

"Lake."

"Good, that's healthy. Panoramic views cleanse the memory."

"I hadn't noticed."

We avoided each other's glance for a minute, and then it became clear that elaboration was required.

"My wife wore ballet slippers around the house, so she was always startling me."

"And?"

"I miss that." Julian stifled a fake yawn. "Ginelle never asked me to leave. She let me figure out for myself what had to be done. She wouldn't reply when I used the word 'our' or referred to a future event: 'Do you want to go the Dells for the Fourth again this year?' If I repeated myself, she'd fix me with an exasperated stare."

"Eventually, the drift was caught."

"Bags packed."

"Yours, naturally, since the house belonged to her family. Luckily, that's about it in terms of assets. This would be the time to disclose any further holdings."

"Nothing," I said. "No, nothing." I did a little twist in my chair, trying to feel the envelope in my pocket.

"You okay?"

"Sure, just getting adjusted."

"It's a big adjustment," Julian said. "Let me just run through the facts of the marriage again. We need to submit an affidavit. You met in 2010. You led a spartan existence, dedicated to science, and she distracted you."

"It may have been a spare existence, but it wasn't spartan. I took all my meals in restaurants and spent most of the rest of my free time in the movies."

"A bachelor has the right to certain indulgences."

"And besides, watching movies helped me push engineering problems to the back of my mind, where they were more likely to get solved. But it went on too long, and I started to notice a pale, shiftless aspect in the mirror. Before loneliness could take root, I went on a serious grooming binge and bought all new clothes for myself."

"A man has to dress for today's corporate environment," he acknowledged.

"Right, Ginny and I were always on the same page about that."

"Same page? You're not even in the same book."

"Anyway, I looked great but felt ridiculous in a wardrobe of new tailored clothes, and the discomfort forced me to be more outgoing than usual."

"You met Ginelle at work."

"We met on the elevator." I was entering Drixa's offices when a scent chiropractically readjusted something that lay deep within me. As I passed through a revolving door, it captivated me like no other sensory experience ever had. Something within the scent faded while something else arrived, all at once; the undertone became the overtone. It was a message just for me, a molecular code. I quickly determined who had used the door four people before I did. Her. She, that brunette, had occupied the same quadrant. With some effort I gained on her as we approached the elevator, all the while scheming frantically, in case I managed to ride up in the same car as she. Her stride was wide.

"What is the fascination with women in elevators?" Julian asked. "Or is it the only time you ever get close enough?"

"There's this movie," I said. "Nobody remembers, but it's a classic moment. The hero boards the elevator with a gorgeous woman, and the second the doors close, they start kissing passionately. Then the doors open, and she gets out."

"Not a word exchanged."

"Exactly. Quite possibly the hero wears a mustache."

"Peter Sellers?"

"No. Did I say 'passionately'? That's not quite it. It's more playful, like a dance they both know."

"David Niven?"

"I don't think so."

"Why are we talking about this, Hayden?"

"When something happens that people don't understand, they say it's like a movie," I said. "When people watch a movie they don't understand, they complain that it's not realistic."

"And all this falls somewhere in between."

"Right," I answered, relieved to be understood.

"You said something on this up elevator with Ginelle."

"If it matters, she spoke first. She'd been hired by the company to interview every employee and compose a short profile. Our interview took place right there and then. She asked what I did, and I said I designed the filters."

—And?

—And drains.

—Do you get much out of that?

—You'd be surprised at what drains catch these days.

She'd smiled with one eye, or with a twitch beside it. The rest of her face betrayed nothing as her hand reached up to the back of her head, as if to adjust the tuning on her bun, and a silver pin sprung loose. It flew upward—I imagined a springing sound, or rather an unspringing—before dropping to the elevator floor. Without realizing what I was doing (or what she was), I fielded the pin expertly, scooping it in my right hand on the first bounce and raising the prize over my head. A dozen thoughts chased each other like freight cars whipping around a bend:

1. Triumph (I caught it)
2. Shame (You caught me)
3. Self-consciousness (I must look like a fool to all these people)
4. . . . and to you
5. I look like the Statue of Liberty
6. There's a rare play, isn't there? In football, when the quarterback holds the ball up like this, waiting for the tailback to grab it.
7. What are the odds that you'd drop the pin at exactly the right moment?
8. How does a pin like this work? Why does bunching hair together hold it in place? Is there really a spring, or is it a hinge?
9. Are you smiling at me like that because you're impressed?
10. Embarrassed?
11. Irked?
12. Did you do that on purpose?

An instant later her hand touched mine—a touch that simultaneously went through me and took something away—and worked the pin out from my grip, and my mind froze and the blood took over, becoming a separate organ wiser and more alert than the mind. I became conscious of physical states other than solid, liquid, and gas.

I understood what scent was. The blood soon returned to my body, but it was chemically different, like water that has cooled a nuclear reactor.

Her smiles grew, spreading first to the other eye and finally down her face. I cherished those moments. I'd got one out of her a couple weeks before our wedding day when I'd bit my tongue in a fudge shop. The only time since then was when I'd stepped on a nail in a furniture warehouse. But not all of Ginelle's smiles had been sadistic, just the ones that came fastest. She had also liked to learn new things and was especially hungry for science. Once I had taught her how to tell a moth from a butterfly; later, I had demonstrated Newton's physics principles using black olives. After a few seconds to process what she'd heard, she'd grinned like a banana.

"The courtship breezed along," I summarized. "And then marriage, a kid, what I'd thought was a life."

"Well," Julian breathed—not so much satisfied with my account as relieved that it was over—"you had a pretty good marriage for quite a while, as durable as most people can expect. You had the house in Kenwood, the kid, the worries, the vacations. You redecorated together and subscribed to the fall-winter schedule at the ballet. Not my thing, of course. I prefer Vegas, but still, that counts for something. In fact it's better than most can say. The thing to do now is let go of all that and get out of the way."

"I didn't expect Ginelle to be awarded full custody of the kid at the pretrial hearing."

"Things turned out better than expected, *considering*."

"I don't know what you mean." Actually, I did and I didn't.

That is, I had to find out what he knew, what she knew, so I sat on my hands and tried to listen without objecting.

"Let's review the history, Hayden. Ginelle goes on a trip and you get . . . "

"Some help, domestic help."

"That's one way of seeing it. Let me tell you how this Snowflake Lodge looks to the judge. You marry this great-looking woman, use her up, and then send her away like it's all her idea."

"Well, I don't know if *use* . . . Anyway, it's important to say that Ginelle went away first. She recommended the Snowflake Lodge. She said I couldn't take care of Hayden Jr. and myself both. It was all her idea."

"Bet you couldn't wait till that plane took off. Beer and beef every night, bacon every morning. Broccoli—never heard of it. The ballet or the Bears game? Hmm, tough call. You got her to carry your baby for nine months, suffer through forty-eight hours of labor, and allow her body to be forever stamped by the experience—all to bring someone into the world with your first and last name. Looks like you, too."

"He does, doesn't he?"

"And now that she's done incubating your clone for you and raised him to the age where he can wipe his own ass, she leaves the continent. You order another girl and start all over again."

Rather than disputing this version of events, I signed the affidavit that Julian had prepared (noticing but not remarking on the terms "mail-order bride" and "pattern of infidelity") and made my getaway. The way I figured, it was better to sign the divorce papers before signing the Letter of Agreement. Then if the promotion and, presumably, raise did come through, I wouldn't be compelled to share.

The parking lot reminded me of the moon's surface. The moon reminded me of a streetlight. Under a tarpaulin, five human forms sat among three cardboard fortresses. They made no sound, beside the occasional complaint in a dead language. Chicago still had neighborhoods, but they were less neighborly now and more hivish. I didn't know what these insectoid people did for sustenance except that it must have been grim.

According to some estimates, the homeless population approached, or had already eclipsed, the number of people with homes. A parallel society had arisen, or a nonsociety free of law.

I started the other way, down a path between two piles of rust-colored stone back toward the hotel. It was not a far walk, but it took me over a stretch of crags and a vacant lot cross-hatched with fallen trees just west of Halsted. A catnap amidst the sweet rot of stumps sounded good about now, but I lumbered on, feeling some-what absent from the plot but not especially caring.

Could a Hayden Shivers biopic be made without Hayden Shivers? If I wound up on the cutting room floor, what difference would it make? When the credits rolled at the end, would my name appear?

Chapter Four

The phone in my jacket pocket went off, and, blinking dumbly, I pressed the answer button before remembering that it wasn't my phone.

"Mr. Dawson, I'm glad I reached you."

"*Who* has reached me?" I imitated.

"Shoals. Warne Shoals. I'm calling from the *Tribune*'s Utility section. You've probably skipped us a thousand times."

"They put you between Jobs and Real Estate. It's a tough slot."

"Exactly. We're doing a special section in honor of the kickoff, and Drixa gave me this number to fact-check our science. Can I read something to you?"

"This isn't really a good time."

"It'll only take a minute."

"A minute." That was just how Lionel would say it. Striking the chord that combined *I doubt you could do it in a minute* and *a minute is all you get*.

He read:

How Drixa Did It
By Warne Shoals
You cannot understand the genius that went into Drixa's new top-secret synthetic water substitute, expected to debut this week in homes across Chicagoland, without first understanding the luck.

For years, Drixa has thrived in the highly competitive water industry, weathering regulation, population shifts on a scale never before witnessed in this country, and environmental calamity requiring expensive new filtration technologies, but experts have long maintained that nothing short of radical innovation could guarantee the continuation of this winning streak.

After all, there's only so much pure water left. Except for a few million gallons a year from costly subcrust mining operations, the limit is fixed. Ironclad. Seawater was the great murky hope for years, but desalinization remains slow and costly.

Here's where the luck comes in. It started the day an unnamed Drixa researcher set out to collect samples on Fungus Rock, an unremarkable Mediterranean outcropping off the coast of Malta. All he was trying to do was to supercharge the charcoal in a filter, but when he tested the fungus (technically, a parasitic flowering plant, a brilliant pink-orange when crushed), the results puzzled him: more water came out of the filter than had gone into it.

Splash, the world was wet again. But first, a deal had to be negotiated with the Maltese, and within days of the discovery, Lionel Dawson was signing papers with the Prime Minister. Details of the agreement have been closely guarded, but sources hint at an unprecedented figure. Don't be surprised if the Maltese standard of living shoots through the roof.

"When does this run?" I asked.

"You tell me."

"I wouldn't know, you'd have to ask the Chief Engineer." I was feeling just confident enough and figured the less said, the better.

"Can you put me in touch?"

"I'll be sure to get back to you on that."

"Where did he get the idea?"

"Who?"

"Aren't we talking about the Chief Engineer?"

"What makes you think it was his idea?"

"For background purposes only," he promised. "How did the idea come about? Whoever had it, it had to come from somewhere."

The bluff would probably leave me fired and humiliated. In the voice of Lionel Dawson, I could style Hayden Shivers a latter-day Galileo, with a dash of inventrepreneurship, but for every proof that the world is round there are a thousand crackpot patents collecting dust and grudges. "From what I understand," I began, "It's easier to ask where it didn't come from . . . It wasn't a gut instinct or a calculated hypothesis. It wasn't a dream or a sudden revelation in the bathtub. It didn't come suddenly or gradually. It didn't give pleasure or pain when it first appeared."

"No labor pains?"

"It just stood there fully grown, waiting to be recognized. Or remembered," I continued. "Or no, not remembered, but found through forgetting."

"Forgetting what?"

"Basic principles of physics, for starters. Doesn't conservation of matter mean anything to you?"

"Chief Engineer," he whistled. "Whoever it is would have had to sign the agreement." Hearing how that caught my attention, he continued, "Wonder who the sucker is. A lot of people could use that formula besides Drixa."

"Warne, I'm going to have to call you back." The wind picked up in front of the Brahms, carrying with it the engine sound from the waterworks and the alkaloid scent of stalled traffic. I didn't bother to ask again about the room upgrade and made my way through the sanctified atrium to the elevator, thinking about the movies: who starred in that picture? The one where the hero kisses a stranger in the elevator.

"Forget something?" My diaphragm bucked as Miyumi Park stabbed me in the kidney with the rolled-up envelope containing the Letter of Agreement. She stuffed it into my jacket pocket, patted me on the chest—inclining her head for a chiding kiss I did not accept—and followed me to my room.

Her loyalties were beyond reproach. She was a Drixa partisan through and through; if you cut her she'd bleed pure icewater. Yet I do believe she liked me. Knowing her reasons would probably bring pain, but the look of affection she'd given me was genuine, and even if I didn't believe every word she'd said, I still trusted her. There is something unaccountably pleasant about putting your trust in the untrustworthy. Stupid, maybe, but nonetheless pleasant, like getting drunk on champagne.

We sat on the bed closest to the window, between us a plate of chilled shrimp, lemon wedges, and assorted nuts and cheese that she'd ordered. "I won't bother describing the time I had spent immersed in the basement lab," I told her as I withdrew the cheese knife from a brick of sharp cheddar. "A period of years when my chief activity beyond the workweek consisted of somewhat arbitrary trials with a limited yet maddening set of variables. To describe the activity would be to miss the point, and besides, it's boring."

"No!" she insisted with her professionally affectionate conde-scension.

"What is it called that happens to deep-sea divers? They rise from the depths too quickly, and painful air bubbles form in the bloodstream. Or maybe it's more comparable to the sensation we all have when we emerge blinking and dazed in the cinema parking lot, except that it felt more or less permanent."

"Where's the filter," she asked.

"It has bugs."

"Don't worry. There's a whole team of engineers to work those out."

"The bends. That's the word."

That seemed to lay the subject to rest for the moment. Out of extreme self-consciousness or utter lack of it, one or the other, I decided it was a good time to demonstrate the principle of the catapult. I asked Miyumi to hurl a peanut at the window as hard as she could. It barely made a ping.

"Try again, throw it harder this time."

"How about a shrimp?"

"Even better. Remember, with all your might."

The shrimp slapped the window and dropped behind a chair.

"Now," I instructed. "Do you see what I have here? Nothing extraordinary, no gunpowder or other explosives, right? Just a hand towel, a shoe tree, and my braces," I said unhooking them from my pants.

Miyumi looked dubious.

"Okay, here we have a primitive catapult. Load a peanut in there and gently pull back. Gently. Now let go!" There was a thwack on the far wall, and a spot where the paint was gone from the wall.

"Hayden Shivers!" she exclaimed, this time loading a shrimp and aiming it at me. I ducked and—bang! A two-inch crack appeared in the window.

Stepping toward the bathroom, she switched over to flattery. "I can't believe that water as we knew it has come to an end." She poured a glass from the faucet. The sign above said:

Nonpotable!

"That may be how you sell it," I said. "But look at the history. Late in the twentieth century, somebody predicted that 'the next world war' would be fought over water. Newspapers regularly issued warnings of mass dehydration and exfoliation, like something out of the Book of Revelations. The war never came."

"Yeah, but the hydrocrisis carved the globe up as effectively as any war, with corporations redrawing national borders in accordance with pipelines."

"People will always need water to drink. This isn't a rupture with history; it's a continuation."

"People used to drink tap," Miyumi recalled. "We sucked tap ice cubes and mixed tap lemonade without boiling first. We gargled with the stuff. Nowadays people are afraid to give it to their cats or let their goldfish swim in it."

"Drixa filters water. That's not going to change. 'Unfiltered' still belongs to the barbarians of Europe. In boardrooms and law offices across the country, what do they call behavior and ideas that should have been left in the last century? Unfiltered. On college campuses, it's the ultimate putdown. Just about the only Americans who still drink unfiltered water are members of shock performance troupes who probably fake it, and ICE-9 collective, who only go unfiltered a few times a month, under careful medical supervision."

"Some people have expressed doubts about them."

Particles swirled in the glass she held. I was expected to concur.

Technically, ICE-9 still belonged to the scientific consortium Independent Council on the Environment. Unrelenting damage to the water and the air forced them to radicalize their agenda. But a lot of respected commentators had been saying that they had departed so far from their initial charter that they had effectively become a new animal. Current and former members were forever squabbling in the Opinion page of the *Tribune*.

"Let's see that filter, Hayden."

"All I have is the prototype," I explained. "And there's a problem with the prototype."

"Which is?"

"Which is it's missing." To allay her disappointment, I unzipped my duffel. "But I have some fungus you can see." I pulled out a small tupperware bowl and lifted the lid with a *thwop*, revealing a handful of orange-pink granules the consistency of roquefort.

"Has the *Tribune* seen this?" she said, taking a pinch and rubbing it into powder. "They would love a shot of this."

"They haven't called me, I haven't called them," I assured her, still conscious of being tested. "Put the glass down on the dresser and mark the level with something." She pulled out a hotter shade of lipstick than I expected and drew a precise dash. "Now we need that bracelet, if you don't mind."

"What else?"

"Some porous fabric." She untied her scarf, leaving a pair of wonderfully naked clavicles. "Nice," I said, "but finer would be better."

"I know what you need," she said, and sat on the bed. She reached down and unbuckled the pump on her right foot. With a single economic motion, her skirt raised up and one black silk stocking slipped off her leg.

"Yes," I said, testing its strength. "Definitely." At first, the powder wouldn't adhere to the fabric, but we found a candle and gently warmed it enough to melt, but not enough to burn. A sweet, ancient odor rose up between us. I wrapped the coated stocking around the bracelet and sent Miyumi to fetch a second glass. Then I poured the water from one to the other through the fabric and set the one with the lipstick mark on the dresser. But first I jiggled the glass the best I could. "There," I said. "I've done better, but that's something. Probably not enough, though." The water was barely a centimeter higher than the mark on the glass—actually a better result than I had expected. At this point, I wouldn't have understood how the candle helped.

"Not even for an honorary first sip?" She put the glass in my hand. The smell was less sulfurous than it had been originally, and when I sloshed the water it didn't leave any residue on the inside of the vessel. I counted to twenty as the particles settled. Her bare leg had a kind of matte finish. Her unpainted toes were nearly all the same size.

"Hayden, it's wonderful. We're going to do it just like that at the launch. You'll take the first sip in front of all the reporters and dignitaries. There'll be a polite round of applause. You'll smile modestly."

"Of course."

" . . . before collapsing in a heap before them all."

"Pardon?"

"Oh, I think you understand."

"You want me to sip and fall. "

"Yes, in that order."

"To show how safe it is to drink the product."

"Exactly."

The leg was magnificent, both as an anatomical specimen and as a tool of persuasion. I struggled to put up the slightest bit of resistance. "Let's say I drink but don't fall."

"Oh, I don't think it works without the fall. We're going for an event here, something memorable. Unexpected. Which Lionel says is the same thing."

"Okay, but what are they going to remember, the sip or the fall?"

"We can get someone else, Hayden," she groaned. Or was it a moan?

"Another inventor? . . . No, it's okay, I'll do it." Closing my eyes, I drank from the glass. The muscles in my throat spasmed momentarily, but I drained the whole thing down.

"Lionel will be so pleased. You could sign the letter now, and we'll be on our way."

"What's it called?" I asked. "Does it have a name yet?"

She reached into her pocketbook and handed me a trifold brochure. On the cover, there was an artfully blurred photo of a pair of hands cupping rainwater.

H_2O = water

On each successive page, similar shots illustrated a series of short poems.

dancing in the rain
we never knew each other better
never cared so much before
never cared so much again
as during that spontaneous disco
that night in the backyard
after dinner
and before the dishes
—rachel i., dubuque

Trembling, I wiped my mouth and started babbling about my son, my little boy. "He can grow up now or he can grow up later. I say, put it off a few years. Go on living in this trusting, kind, though altogether false world as long as you can. Seven years old and he still thinks cartoons are real! Of course they're more realistic than they were when we were kids. We did watch a lot of cartoons back then."

crying in the shower
the lights out, the phone dead
in a friendless country
the only words i understood
were the tears on my cheeks
the water coursing down my body
and the smell of hotel soap
—rae f., rockford

"'Comics,' Dad called them," I said, ignoring Miyumi's leg. I continued to read the poems.

washing delicates in the sink
the machine is fine for some things
but not my favorite pants.
a clean sink filled with lukewarm water
fine fabric wash
and five minutes
wring, rinse, and wring again
gently, though, please
then dry it in the wind
—tony z., rock island

this gift was made possible by hydrogen & oxygen
and drixa & you
please recycle

Miyumi checked her watch, with its delicate gold-chain bracelet and small ivory face and hands as skinny as eyelashes, while I strained to get a reading without getting any closer. "Maybe he's better off never knowing the difference," I alleged, sitting very still as the city's glare assaulted me through tinted glass.

"Won't the fact that I'm on the floor arouse some concern?"

"For you?" she smiled, pulling off the other stocking.

"About the product."

Miyumi put her shoes back on and headed for the door. "You're the inventor, right? And you're the one drinking, right? That's all they want to know."

CHAPTER FIVE

Chewed tails of cocktail shrimp were scattered about the hotel room, wineglasses with dark sediment, pillows without pillowcases on the floor, sheets twisted. I called downstairs, then thought twice, realizing it might be an awkward thing to complain about, but a helpful voice answered before I could put the receiver down.

"The maid, has she done the eleventh floor yet?"

"No, my apologies, sir. I'll send someone up as soon as possible."

"Thanks, just tell her to skip my room today. Everything is fine here."

"Will you be requiring anything at all? A snack? A bowl of ice cream?"

"I couldn't, I just ate at Giorgio & Gina's."

"Right," the voice said. "The cows."

I bent over to pick up a stocking stained orange with fungus. Held up to the glass, it revealed the city's tarnished shimmer, the financial citadels, the ballpark, extinguished streetlamps lining the backward-flowing river. I held it before me whispering Miyumi's name. Her musk still clung to it. Light perspiration, exultation, and the distillation of natural and synthetic essences.

Stashing it would be heartless, yet every horizontal surface in the room was covered with detritus of our encounter. A melted candle clung to the top of the dresser like a barnacle. A small bowl of cocktail sauce spilled across the top of the cabinet that held the television set. Wadded napkins, dirty silverware, cufflinks, peanut shells, and lemon rinds littered every inch.

Suddenly there was a sound, the sharp crack like a mousetrap snapping that made me gasp. Heart whirring, I whirled and saw the tiny and perfectly round hole in the glass curtain wall facing the river. Another perfectly round hole had somehow pierced the opposite wall.

Probably it was just one of those stray bullets. Most shootings these days were random. Stray bullets punctured lungs, eyes, arteries indiscriminately and without warning. It was better that way, like a reverse lottery.

I decided to clean the room myself. In the sink, I mixed a solution of complimentary shampoo, aftershave, and mouthwash with juice from a lemon wedge and used it on a wool sock to polish every surface to a shine. I scraped the candle wax off the dresser, using the unserrated side of the cheese knife to avoid nicks. I pressed the sheets using an iron from the closet and made the beds. Somehow, my watch had ended up on the floor behind the toilet. The whole process took nearly two hours, but I found it very satisfying, even crawling around on the carpet picking up peanut shells and shrimp fragments with my bare fingers.

Now the hotel room was the cleanest it had been in seventy, eighty years. I had told myself that opening the Letter of Agreement was not permitted until the room was spotless, and when this moment came I sat on the edge of the bed with great anticipation, but the letter was missing from my jacket pocket. I tried my pants, then went over to the closet in case something in there would jog a memory. Because that's what you do when you lose things. You check the closet. Of course, there was nothing there or under the bed or on the dresser. I had just cleaned it all off. It wasn't in a drawer or either wastebasket. Losing things always panicked me. A cool, greasy perspiration covered every inch of skin, accompanied by shortness of breath, a stream of muttered curses.

Why was it so much worse to lose things than to get lost? I tried gazing through the window, but all I noticed were the reflection of the room and all the places·I still needed to search.

I went back to the jacket. Not only was the letter missing, but the phone too. Lionel's phone. It was a distinct possibility that my conversation with the reporter had been a setup, but had I lost the written promise of my promotion as well?

The idea of retracing steps repulsed me, but its logic was undeniable. In preparation, I started down the hallway to get some ice for my burning forehead, and there was the envelope, on the floor outside.

We are pleased to invite you to the Grand Opening of Our Municipal Waterworks. As a Member of the Engineering Corps that brought the Project to Fruition, you will be introduced by the CEO at a Press Reception preceding the Event. We hope you won't mind answering Reporters' questions about the Project. In addition, please provide a Short Biography of yourself for the Press Packet.

Thank you from your friends at Drixa.

Please note that signing this biographical statement indicates your agreement to the conditions of employment at Drixa, whereby any and all patents, awards, royalties, and reimbursements earned as a chief-level Drixa manager belong exclusively to the Drixa Corporation in perpetuity.

A real drink was required to sort things out. I folded the letter, changed into a shirt that matched the gray sky, and took the elevator down. No beautiful women materialized when the doors parted.

The lobby was full of Zodia people headed for rendezvous of some kind. An excessively handsome junior executive threw his arm around his pudgy boss. Three women were arguing over who would pay their bar tab. The Pepper Mill's host was laughing out of all proportion at a casual remark made by the elder of two soon-to-be pensioners. It reminded me of the wisdom of appealing to crass motives like profit, publicity, and politics. I exhorted myself to *think* crass, and who should spring to mind but Julian Dameron. The guy had upheld crassness as his professional creed. I dialed his number. "Glad you caught me," he said. "The move is going all right, *considering*. But it's taking longer than expected." It sounded like he was eating hard candy.

"Who's moving?" I asked.

"Ginelle has decided to leave you the house," Julian said. The tone suggested he was reminding me, when in fact this was the very opposite of what we had discussed earlier.

"I'll stay here again tonight," I offered. "Tell Ginelle not to worry about it. Moving's a bitch."

"Good one."

"I didn't mean that," I protested. "Now you're going to tell her I said that."

"Don't worry, she's almost packed, but the kid's toys are all over the place, the bed frame isn't coming apart, and the truck showed up two hours early and refused to wait."

"I said I'd stay here tonight," I said, picturing my wife and my lawyer filling cardboard boxes with books. Julian had probably won Hayden Jr.'s affection with ease. It didn't take much to charm the boy—a coin trick, pig latin, twenty questions, and he was yours.

"Julian, what are you doing in the house?"

"I'm here on your behalf,"

"So it's costing me . . . "

"It's saving you, having someone here, overseeing matters and representing your interests."

"Can I talk to her?"

"I wouldn't recommend it."

"Would you put Hayden Jr. on?"

"I would, but." He didn't bother finishing the sentence. He probably just didn't feel like letting the boy handle his phone, but leaving the explanation unsaid gave it an import I dared not challenge.

"I have something I want to show you," I said. "Can we meet?"

"How long will it take you to get to the Justice Complex?"

"By car, thirty minutes."

"And on foot?"

"I don't know, about the same."

Somewhere above, an alarm went off, a dirty buzz-buzz-buzz, and I leapt up from the barstool, proceeded in an orderly fashion toward the exit, and stood on a patch of lawn outside, squinting up at the hotel, waiting for everybody else to emerge.

"See you in thirty minutes," Julian said.

"Sure," I answered.

"Ten forty-five," Julian said. "Will you remember that?"

"I think so."

"All right," he said. "Just checking."

Nobody followed me outside, even though the alarm was still going.

A grassy pathway led away from the hotel, under Michigan Avenue and along the river. To judge from the seams between bolts of sod, it must have been recently planted.

Somebody had left a newspaper box open, and I pulled a copy out.

Questions Emerge About Drixa's New Product

Drixa Director Lionel Dawson admitted in an interview yesterday that "the basic principles of physics" had been forgotten by the researcher who pioneered the method for generating its new synthetic water substitute, H_2O. Whether the cause of the scientist's amnesia had yet been confirmed was not clear at press time.

Pamela Barbarossa, Senior Fellow at the University of Chicago Medical School's Neurology Department, confirmed that such effects are possible, while cautioning that no conclusions could yet be drawn. "It is well established," she said, "that isotopes of familiar compounds, if that's what we're dealing with, may cause deleterious reactions quite distinct from the common configuration of, for example, water."

Drixa plans to launch H_2O at a public ceremony on a date to be announced shortly. Mayor King is expected to attend. Calls to his office about whether his plans have changed in light of the revelations about amnesia were not returned.

The lawn turned spongy beneath my feet as I figured how soon Miyumi would determine who had given Shoals an interview and how futile my excuses would sound. True, my Lionel was flawless, and I hadn't said anything he wouldn't have, but being taken out of context isn't the real problem if you don't belong in the context to begin with.

My legs continued to work without receiving signals from my distracted brain, and they carried me down Dearborn alongside a convoy of stalled school buses. Lit from behind, an enormous photo-realist painting of a glass tumbler sweated in the glow of an ideal dawn, surmounted by the message H_2O = Water.

A cadre of protestors milled in front of the Drixa facility, sharing tea from a chrome thermos and decorating their barricades with signs and POLICE LINE tape. They stood in an unwitting formation, the space between any two protestors and their arrangement across the lot determined by a law more powerful than gravity—the law of futility. In their fatigued postures and unexpectant stares, they betrayed their faithlessness in the right of assembly. Up close, it was a markedly attractive group, even wholesome. All the protestors seemed to really like each other, and when a car slowed down, they patiently explained their cause to the driver, raising their voices only to be heard above the plant's roar.

"They're synthesizing fake water in there."

"What's fake? Two hydrogens and one oxygen is water. Real water."

"See the river? That's water. Where does that come from?"

"From the Great Lakes, I guess, only they're not so great any-more."

"And where does the water in the lake come from?"

"Look, I get what you're saying, I just don't care where it comes from as long as it goes splish-splash."

A security guard kept a bored eye on two young men on stilts performing an accordion duet. One of the female protestors deco-rating the barricade looked up when her ponytail came undone, and she spotted me. I didn't look away quickly enough. "Look who's here," she called out to the others. Even at night and from a distance of twenty feet, I could see that her eyes were violet. The color held me so tight that I didn't notice the other protestors enfolding me as I approached the barricade. They kept very quiet—respectful, nervous, giddy before their visitor. The guard shrugged at nobody in particular.

When she spoke, everything else grew even quieter. "You had to show up eventually, didn't you?" she said, tying her thick black hair behind her head. "If I knew this was the night I would have made a special effort."

"You look fine," I said, trying to sound as mechanically hand-some as Harrison Ford.

"I'm not talking about me, I'm talking about this." She took a length of police tape and wound it around her hand.

"I'm not sure I'm supposed to be here, either, Miss . . ." I studied the color contrast between the ribbon and her tanned skin.

"Come closer," she whispered. "Call me Aqua. Lady Miss Aqua Bella if you care to be formal." Somebody handed me a cup of tea in a paper cone. It tasted minty yet earthy.

"Get him a T-shirt," someone said, and I was handed a white shirt with the slogan TEST THE WATERS printed on it.

"You've shown real dedication, Miss Aqua," I said. "Your mes-sage is really getting out there. What are you going to do now?"

"I don't know, take a swim in the river, probably."

"You can't swim in the river."

"Oh, I can swim there. We all do it. All you've got to do is dive in."

"Dive in?"

"Get used to it. The whole city's going under."

The knot of protestors remained hushed, but I could feel the heat of their attention, particularly the gaze of an innocent-faced but badly shaved student wearing three jackets of different colored denim, committing me to memory.

"What else?" I asked.

"I drink straight from the tap, without a cup." When she saw I didn't have anything to say to that, she continued: "I form my hands into a bowl and slurp it up with my tongue like a wildcat. It streams down my forearms and drips off my elbows." She stretched her arms out to emphasize their shapeliness.

"I should mosey," I said, making the kind of absurd word choice that I only made in the presence of female beauty. Who was I, John Wayne? "But the reason I'm here is to say I'll do whatever I can to help." It occurred to me that the barricades served both the company and the protestors, and I wondered who put them up.

"You'll help. Who will *you* help?"

When the student in the denim jackets finally spoke, his voice was surprisingly delicate, like something aged in the desert. At first the words wouldn't emerge, just a wheezy stammer. "Mr. Shivers," he said, "it is a great honor to us who knowing you. We make documentary film, yes?"

"No documentaries, please," I complained. "And what are you talking about?"

The student's words, though barely audible over the wind, held my attention. "Water is simple, but yet, not simple." His lips writhed with the effort of forming language. "You drinking water, Mr. Shivers, I drinking water, yet Drixa water won't never be pure. Too much things in this water. Too much! So much millions dollars for advertisements! In this water. So many people saying on the

TV, 'This good water. This bad water.' Too much information, Mr. Shivers. The body is not liking this. Information is like . . . like fluoride. Too much, very poison."

"That's enough, Varuk," said Aqua Bella. "Our demands are straightforward: more testing is needed before the launch of the product—independent testing, independent of the so-called Independent Council on the Environment and every other Drixa- or government-sponsored bureau. We're on a round-the-clock vigil to hopefully disrupt the next delivery of Maltese fungus."

Another protestor inserted herself. "My problem is, where are they getting the oxygen? Don't we need oxygen to breathe? Having enough water to drink is fine and dandy, but not at the price of mass suffocation. What will happen when the oxygen runs out?"

"Drixa will start packaging it."

"And selling it on a subscription basis!"

A pair of headlights turned us all into shadow puppets, and Miyumi Park jumped out of the backseat of the company car. She approached us sternly smiling, her command of the situation no less authentic for being practiced. "I see you've met before I could introduce you. Lionel's sorry he couldn't make it."

"Too busy saving the world from tap water," Aqua sneered.

"A number of independent studies have confirmed the threat," Miyumi answered. "You know that. This project is a top priority for Mayor King. Drixa regards its partnership with Chicago as sacred, and we're delighted that Hayden Shivers has agreed to take part in Friday's launch."

"This Friday?" I said.

"Oh, sure," Aqua said, mocking my surprise.

"Friday, March 4," Miyumi confirmed.

"We'll be there," Aqua said.

"What exactly are you going to launch this Friday?" I asked.

"Hayden, we discussed this." I let her stuff me in the backseat and tenderly stroke my head. "You look tired," she said after about thirty strokes. I craned my neck, but Aqua had already turned away.

"I'm fine."

Miyumi had surprised me in the elevator with the Letter of Agreement, but most of the time I couldn't help feeling that I was the one catching her off guard. She'd be rattling off policies and positions in a metallic voice stamped by three years of graduate school in industrial relations when she'd look up at the prescribed moment to make eye contact and a shadow would pass over her eyes as she realized the inconsequence of her quarry. Her mouth would slacken to a cursive o, which she would expertly suppress a tenth of a second later. But there it was. The o reappeared quite predictably, each time vanishing before the rest of the exclamation could be expressed, but we both knew it was, *oh, it's only you*. I'd smile crookedly, she'd blush, and the moment would pass. It was almost flirtation, and I tried not to take it as an insult.

"We can still get you into the Executive Suite tonight. Down pillows, down quilt, 300-count sheets. Fluffy white robes you can take home with you." She tugged gently at the t-shirt on my lap. "I said I'm fine, I just have an appointment." The inside of the car felt cramped and sweaty, and the windows were caked with water spots and ochre dust. Every time Lucluc braked I got an elbow of nausea in the gut.

Miyumi had gone for an elaborate and unflattering manicure. Marbleized patterns of mother of pearl and lavender swirled at the end of her fingers, making her hands look less feminine than before. The worst part was that it was clearly intended to please somebody else. Toxic fumes hung glamorously in the back of the cab, recycling through the ventilation system and stinging my eyes. On her lap she held a pocketbook of freshly killed leather.

We weren't going anywhere, just driving in a wide circle, adding to the traffic. Miyumi hummed tunelessly but with enthusiasm, gave me a hungry smile, and took my hand. The hand felt different now, but I didn't mind as long as I didn't have to look at it, so I focused on a billboard advertising Rainforest Daytrips.

"You're doing great with everyone on the hiring committee,"

she finally said. "But don't push your luck. She's quicksand. Did you sign the letter yet? I don't have to tell you this is a marvelous career opportunity. I probably shouldn't be telling you this, but at this point it's safe to say that the Chief Engineer decision is just about finalized, and you won't be disappointed."

"Miyumi," I said, clutching the gift from Aqua. "It's not ready yet. What you're calling H_2O is just an observation I've been toying with, just a concept. Somebody's got to explain to those protestors . . . and to the *Tribune* . . . and to Lionel."

She blinked. "You really don't know, do you?"

"I miss a lot when I'm down in my lab."

"But you do know that Lionel and the protestors have their truce, but now is not the best time."

"I must have missed that. I must have been—"

"Down in the lab, I know. Just wait, Hayden. You'll have all the time you need, after the launch. We'll set you up in the best lab possible, give you everything you need. Buckets of fungus. Just help us out first, let's get the word out there, underscore Drixa's commitment to alternative waters. That's what we need to buy you the time you need."

We were on the shoulder now, just a few yards away from the billboard.

SEE ENOUGH NATURE TO LAST A LIFETIME.

I pictured tourists trudging through artfully designed underbrush, desperately capturing the fake scenery in their camcorders. Some would never watch their tapes. Others would edit the footage, dub in appropriately tropical music, and subject their friends to repeated viewings. A small percentage of cameras would malfunction, and there would be discussions to decide if a second trip were in order.

I turned back to her. "Your faith in the process is appreciated. It's real, it just needs more time."

"Your confidence is encouraging," she said. "Especially since we're introducing it on Friday."

"Sip and fall," I said, still believing that they had assigned me the role of martyr. It wasn't such a stretch, at least not in my imagination.

"Correct." Miyumi nodded to the driver, and the car spun around, wobbling like a toy as it climbed back onto the road. In the mirror, Lucluc's thick mustache barely concealed a nervous smile. Miyumi clapped along to invisible music, trying to show how much fun she was having.

"That's a cool shirt you put on. What color do you call that?" She kept using the word cool.

"Gray. Just gray," I said, getting out.

"Come on, it definitely has some heather in it. Did your wife pick it out?"

"No, well, yes. She gave me a choice of two, and I picked this one."

"That's a cool way to do it."

I yanked the handle. "Thanks for the ride."

"Hayden," Miyumi called out. "Don't forget walk-through is tonight."

"Right," I answered, though the concept wasn't the least bit familiar.

CHAPTER SIX

It would be a brief conversation. Ninety percent of Julian Dameron's attention focused on a glass bowl upon a rolltop desk, in which an angelfish swam tight circles.

"How's he doing?" I asked.

"How's who doing?"

"Him," I said, tapping the bowl.

"I'm not looking at the fish," Julian sneered catatonically. "I'm looking at what the fish is swimming in."

"Julian, why are you looking at the water?"

"It's not water," he responded. "It's H_2O."

"Where did you get it?"

"Free sample. The Justice Complex received a few gallons this afternoon as a special offer." That was more than I had ever generated in my basement.

"You want some lemonade or something?" he asked. "A long vacation, maybe?"

"What, I'm burned out, you're saying?"

"It's not for me to judge. Burnout? The term has no bearing. Have you given up trying? On the contrary. The thing you're doing with your face is, well, effortful."

"And what do you think it is that I'm trying to do?"

"Again, not my call. As your lawyer, I'm a mouthpiece. I say what you tell me to say, only better."

"Effortful."

"You're doing it right now. Try to let the tension go, Hayden. No, that's even worse; you still look like you're trying to remember something: it just slipped away, and you're scrambling to get it back. Am I warm?"

"I suppose it could be something like that."

"That feeling when you first wake up and you look around to establish you are where you thought you were. It's one thing in the morning, but if it recurs over the course of the day, that's a problem."

"It's what ICE-9 has been saying."

"They hear that memory is affected and they call it amnesia. This is subtler, even sublime. It's a mental habit of dissolving the bond between cause and effect. You could watch a nail being driven into a board and deny that the hammer played a part. You could clean all of the ice cream out of the freezer, throw away the carton, and immediately check the freezer for ice cream. Did you 'forget' it was gone, or do you stubbornly maintain that just because it's been eaten doesn't mean it couldn't possibly be there? It's a form of genius, probably."

"What would you say," I asked, "if I told you that I invented H_2O?"

"Did you?"

"Drixa believes that I did. They want me to sign a Letter of Agreement that hands the patent over to them."

The fish's eyes were hot and panicked. It seemed not to be getting enough oxygen through its gills. It knew something funny was going on.

"Going to?"

"It might help me get the Chief Engineer job. What do you think?"

"As your lawyer?"

"Does that mean you'd get a percentage?"

Looking directly through the angelfish, he said, "You want my advice? Drag it out as long enough, and you might end up with more than a promotion."

"That's kind of what I was thinking."

"They use your invention before striking a deal with you, they expose themselves to considerable risk. Think about it. Every drop they're pumping is on loan from you, with the interest not yet established. You could take over the company, but of course . . . "

"What?"

"Say you take over Drixa. Who stands to take over Shivers?"

"Could Ginelle do that?"

"You could have the finest lawyer in town," Julian said, "and you'd still be left out to dry."

"Lucky for me, then, that Drixa isn't pumping H_2O yet. That stuff in the bowl might not even be the real thing."

"I just told you, it's not real, it's H_2O."

"I mean not real H_2O. How do you know it isn't water? I can't even tell for sure."

"Just look at him," Julian said with finality.

In the mood for a shower and a shave, I headed northeast on Ogden, passing a pole with a motorcycle on top, a low building covered in red glitter, and a vast and empty parking lot with billions of glass bits dancing in the intense sunlight of late morning, late winter. Around a mysteriously gleaming-new 2006 Lexus GS 300, below the elevated tracks whose shadows criss-crossed Franklin Street, a group of children in mismatched furs sharpened sticks and decorated rusty oil drums with police tape. They didn't look up when I passed. A graystone from Chicago's glory years, the postfire building boom, had been rescued and repurposed for utility and infrastructure management, before Drixa took water over. Hey, was this *always* Water Street?

Many decades of wingtips had trod the figure out of the rug's center lane; there were as many broken or burned-out fixtures as working; and the paint jobs varied from door to door. At what point do old buildings outlast their charm and fall into decrepitude? A good number of buildings had gone up and come down since this one had reached that stage.

Here was the conference room where the waterbug first bit me. I'd been doodling in the margins of a notebook (doodling was part of the job), while some sort of government official rattled off actuarial calculations.

Expense	($ per million gals.)	Risk (of failure)	Risk (of disaster)
Desalinization	5	.6	.09
Deep drilling	9	.6	.03
Astronomical	17	.4	.14

Desalinization technologies had been around for centuries, but they were inherently inefficient, and if the seawater was contaminated enough, then removing the salt didn't accomplish much. Drilling below the earth's crust for water had seemed promising for a time, but methods of locating veins remained primitive, even superstitious. Professional dowsers had already fleeced Drixa of billions. And astronomical mining had never gone beyond theory. The notion of spearing a dirty snowball as it streaked through outer space would have to wait until inter-planetary transport caught up with science fiction.

It took me eight months to make sense of the message that I'd scribbled in the margin:

water ➡ filter ➡ more water.

It puzzled me that I could have made this note without having the slightest idea of how to accomplish it, yet without this seedling, the idea never would have born its Maltese fruit.

Now, beside a pocked orange door with the number 12 on it in brass, I lingered. It was bordered by doors number 7 and 39. There was a light coming from underneath the orange door, and a sign on it that said "Payroll," and I pushed through to find a pallid young man behind a desk piled with manila folders.

"Perfect timing," he said. "I just got the deleted scenes from *Richter Scale, Ebolathon, Toxic Cloud, Conflagration, Conflagration Replay*, and *Conflagration Triple Play*. Cheap, come on, I'll show you."

"Thanks, I've got all the disaster footage I need," I said, tapping my temple. Like a lot of kids, the payroll clerk made extra cash trafficking censored scenes from disaster flicks. In light of recent events, Mayor King had severely restricted representations of ecological trauma. Special effects were so good and the news so bad that the public couldn't tell them apart anymore and didn't sufficiently respond to government warnings during genuine emergencies. Many of the scenes in the kid's collection weren't from the movies at all, but it was purer than most of the stuff you got on the streets, he explained, dialing up a sampler on the monitor.

I pretended to show an interest, trying to relate to the younger generation by whistling at scenes of the White House blowing up, a ski lodge crashing down a mountainside, a swarm of bees engulfing a South American village, Manhattan in flames, Manhattan infested with giant rats, Manhattan buffeted by tidal waves. Manhattanites rubbing their eyes in agony as the Toxic Cloud envelops them.

"It's one of the best edits I've seen," the kid said. "A lot of care went into the sequencing. I've probably watched this thirty times, and I always get something different out of it. Stuff the original directors never dreamed of."

A pack of golden retrievers, radiated or otherwise altered, descended upon some villagers, including a character actor I recognized as the sidekick in a beloved series of detective films.

"Can I see that Shivers file for a sec?" I casually asked.

"There you go. But I'm closing up in two minutes, so I'll need them back." The kid handed me three overstuffed folders bound in rubber bands. The papers were disorganized, some clearly belonging to other people's files. Ginelle's name was spelled Janelle. A recent document had us down as childless.

Finally, a handwritten memorandum caught my attention.

H_2O and Amnesia

* Tests not conducted under Drixa's auspices are open to many serious concerns about method.

* The terms "amnesia," "disorientation," "erratic behavior," and "paranoia" are so subjective that many scientists do not consider them statistically relevant.

* Memory fails us all. Why blame Drixa?

* Drixa has shown a longstanding commitment to the health of its customers and to the environment. Our record is beyond reproach.

* H_2O = water! Pure and simple.

"Thanks kid, I'll be back." A stale indoor breeze tickled the back of my neck, inviting me to venture further down the corridor in search of a vent. There was a spicy note in the air, so subtle as to suggest both baked goods and deathly rot.

As I advanced, the worn rug became a plush layer of late-vintage nylon, the numbers on the doors regularized, and the scent formed itself into a fake-pine cleaning product. Then it became apparent that the scent was not artificial but emanated rather from a rare urban glade on the other side of an open window too high to climb through. I pushed through a set of doors marked ALARM WILL SOUND (no such luck) and found myself in an empty parking lot. The sky hung low and motionless, resisting wind and emitting no light, all but refusing to fulfill its role as the sky. Perhaps it was insulted. Perhaps the skyscrapers of Chicago had finally given offense. Did anyone out there know what was going on in here? Would there be another water crisis, with rations and riots, like in other countries, or would fresh water rush out of the faucet the next time I turned the knob?

Was it dangerous arrogance that led me to go along with this story of the miracle of H_2O, or was it just the kind of brinksmanship that would sweeten the deal when I finally signed the invention over to Drixa? Invention—if only. At this stage, H_2O was merely an anomaly, an unexplained if statistically insignificant phenomenon.

The river wound through the city like film through a projector. I decided to walk back to the hotel, counting the H_2O = Water signs that lined Division Street. The famous skyline kept its distance like a doctor consulting a beautiful woman about her terminal illness.

Chapter Seven

Sip and fall. What they wanted me to do was simple enough. I was even, it pains me to say now, honored. Up in my room, I found an envelope that had been slid under the door, promising momentary relief from loneliness, even in the form of an itemized bill. But this was better. Inside was a color printout, the layout from a *Tribune* magazine feature. Scrawled across the top were the words:

this story got killed. do you want to be next?

The article was written by Warne Shoals.

The Director and his Daughter: Is Blood Thicker Than Water?

Lionel Dawson is stuck in traffic, but there's no sign of frustration on his creased, slightly sunburned face. "Did you think they'd build a lane special for my car?" he asks, not bothering to arch an eyebrow. He points out the window. "That tower has been there 150 years. It could use a cleaning, but it looks pretty good. It was never the greatest building in Chicago, but it must have some kind of survival instinct, to remain standing after all this time."

Dawson knows something about longevity. As Director and CEO of Drixa Enterprises Worldwide, he has weathered all manner of challenges to his post, all the while steering his corporation toward the future without hesitation.

The legend is familiar to every schoolchild: In the Art

Institute one day, Georgia O'Keeffe's billboard-scaled painting *Sky above Clouds* inspires a lowly but ambitious engineer to conceive of a domestic application for a charcoal filter invented twenty years earlier for a now-shuttered public aquarium. He obtains the original patent and trades it for stock in an appliance manufacturer that faltered when it passed up the chance to get in on the ground floor of the ice cube maker revolution. Financially moribund and casting about for a low-risk, no-research household product, Drixa puts its faith in the filter. The folks in product development run his idea by marketing, and soon there's a home filtration pitcher in the refrigerator of sixty percent of American households. Before you know it, Drixa controls not just water but sizable shares in government contracts for power, emergency services, and mail delivery.

And then there's Aqua Bella. With her loose ponytail and freckled arms, she might be mistaken for a summer camp counselor or a park ranger. Guess again. The daughter of one of the city's most powerful men—and of one of the environment's worst foes, according to some—is a ruthless ecological activist.

Born Annabelle Dawson, she assumed her nom de guerre when she graduated Yale five years ago. Her initial overtures to ICE-9 were rebuffed. "We weren't interested in someone who wanted to target Drixa for purely emotional reasons," states one longtime member who now extols Aqua's "sense of purpose and innate leadership gifts." Indeed, the ranks of the protest group are said to have swelled dramatically as her participation has increased.

"Let me tell you a story about Annabelle," Lionel says. "She probably doesn't want me to tell you this story, but I think it says a lot about the kind of person she is, even though she was only six or seven at the time. There was a company skating party, maybe for Christmas, maybe for the billionth Drixa filter sold, and the child of another employee was crippled, a little boy with lobster claws where feet should be, and yet he wanted to skate, too. Well, guess who spent the entire party holding the little boy's hand?"

"No, not Aqua!" he laughs after a pause. "But she did find another child willing to help the cripple. She's more than a born leader, she's a born delegator."

Other than that, the CEO is characteristically restrained on the subject of his decidedly disloyal daughter, saying, "We agree to disagree. I admire her vehemence, but she's clearly misguided scientifically."

Aqua's reaction this comment bore out the description of her vehemence: "He said that? I shouldn't even dignify that, except to say that the people of Chicago should watch what's coming out of their faucets." She refused to clarify whether this was a warning about the latest filtration advance from Drixa or about the suspected ICE-9 plot to contaminate the water supply.

Questions linger about ICE-9's future. Recent months have seen milder, more constructive tactics as holding informal brunch conferences with an exclusive roster of politicians and business leaders who previously would have been the target of boycotts and sabotage. At the same time, the group is being investigated in a notorious case of petnapping: Bunky, the dachshund of Zodia's CEO Barrett P. Fuss, was grabbed from a backyard in Oak Park and returned only after the company agreed to stop research into a project aimed at converting a million-acre landfill into farmland. Nobody knows how the protestors are financing their increased activity, but ICE-9 insiders deny that Aqua is in any way bankrolling operations.

"They serve a function," Lionel Dawson admits as his car finally reaches its destination. "This is an open society, and we respect that." As he walks away, he adds, "We serve a function, too."

"I have an A. Bella on Water Street," said the operator.

"That's the one."

The candy-coated rasp transmitted with uncanny accuracy over the line. "Aqua Bella."

"Hayden Shivers here."

"Are you coming over, Hayden?"

"How do I find you?" This got a big laugh. Rolling, with perhaps a smutty hum at the bottom. "See you in an hour."

Which left me with an hour to kill. Everyone knows that the nicer a hotel room is, the more depressing it feels alone, late at night, and the Brahms, Chicago's best hotel, was no different. I turned the TV on and then turned it off before the picture even appeared. My whole day had been like television already. It was the twenty-first century, and everything in life aspired to the condition of television, with commercial breaks and programming interchangeable.

From my vantage point on the eleventh floor, the city was legible from left to right—from the congealing mist over the river to the receding contour of the lakefront, from the skid-scrawled cement barrier to the welcome expanse of the expressway and up to the graceful angles of Mies and his disciples. Chicago's grandeur came from the determination long ago that the quickest route should also be the most scenic. Sure, the city had its flaws, but none were visible from up here. This was the philosophical stance I hoped to maintain on sea level.

Shave or read? Eat something? The longer you take to make an inconsequential decision, the less likely it is that it'll be the right one. Then I remembered that the Letter of Agreement had asked for a short biography, which, if I did decide to sign, would be good to have ready.

I found some hotel stationery and a ballpoint. *Educated at the California Institute of Technology, Hayden Shivers has*, I began, then wondered if it was uncouth to mention Cal Tech right away like that.

Hayden Shivers believes that civil engineering
Hayden Shivers is a
Hayden Shivers was born in California. He
Hayden Shivers is a civil engineer. He has designed

I crumpled the paper, but the garbage can was full, so I took it down the hall to dump it in the chute. On the way back, a loud crash came from the room. The sound of somebody dropping down to the floor from an air duct. I checked under the beds and in the closet and bathtub, because that's where you look, but nothing turned up, and I decided something must have thumped the ceiling of the tenth floor. By then my stomach was grumbling.

Which would be less depressing? Eating alone in the Pepper Mill or eating alone in my room? Or simply ignoring the hunger? I decided to brave the restaurant, but of course something went wrong with the elevator. It took me straight down to L, but the doors didn't part. Just then there was a boom in the distance, either a series of small explosions at a slight distance or a reverberating explosion at a great distance, and the lights went dead. I pounded on door with my fist, shouting, "Help! Heyelp!"

In total darkness, I ran at the door from a distance of three feet, smacking shoulder-knees-forehead—damn!—into the steel.
Finally, I found a button that made the doors give a few inches, allowing me to slide my hands between two greasy black gaskets and pry one side back.

Nobody else seemed to be reacting to the explosions, so I attempted to stroll casually into the Pepper Mill and was led to the only empty table. The light was too strong, as if the other patrons—an assortment of invalids with their aides and scared-looking men in their fifties whose tragic prognoses had been confirmed by second and third opinions—needed help getting over jet lag. Service was obsequious yet somehow disdainful. If the bass-fiddle-shaped waiter, carrying the pitcher like a newborn, asked me one more time if I'd care for a refill of lemonade, he was going to get socked in the gut. I ordered lavishly, but by the time the food arrived my hunger had been satisfied by rolls and butter. The steak au poivre stuck out like an iceberg from a murk of blood and grease. When the eponymous pepper came around, not enough came out to make it palatable.

I ventured into the frigid evening. This was the only weather that didn't make my shirt stick to my body. Rolling down Water Street from the lakefront all the way to Michigan Avenue, Drixa's new facility was the largest brick building on record. All of the remaining masons in the city worked on the structure, this architectural embodiment of Lionel's reign over the corporation. It was often said that he designed it himself, but in fact a professional architect was employed, even if he functioned as little more than stenographer. The elevations, the facade, the floor plans, even the oxblood color of the bricks—all 2.2 million of them emblazoned with the trident Drixa logo—were all precisely dictated. Lionel specified the two-foot-thick walls and the simple, elegant sign above the door.

The sign was a decoy. The structure itself was the sign. It said: *Drixa provides safe drinking water*. The much-ballyhooed Vibrational Filtration System for which the building was ostensibly constructed was an utter sham. (I should know; I was shammed into working on it every day for four years.) But the gravity of the brick building and the steady thrum that arose from its core inspired more confidence than any technology real or imagined could have mustered.

At the foot of this cathedral, a few protestors stood around propped against barricades. Three seated figures leaned in toward each other, over a basket containing fruit juice and saltines. Plotting had given way to complaining had given way to private catatonia, and they didn't look up until I was standing right over them.

"She's been waiting for you," one said.

"I thought she'd be here," I answered, not sure whether I was being mistaken for someone else, which was more or less the usual, lately. "Where?"

"Under the bridge. Down there. But it's slippery, watch out in those shoes."

The path to the river's edge led me along the shoulder of an underground expressway, behind an armada of rusting dumpsters, and down a steep incline of loose cinders. Big cities all show their seams over time, areas of lawlessness or abjectness or both. They first appear on the periphery of public works, and the brambles and broken rocks in the shadow of the new waterworks lent this one a haunted, gothic aspect.

In the distance, a small gathering of insectlike people—it was impossible to count them—were striking an upended lemonade machine with golf clubs. Expensive woods, from the sound of it. There was no telling whether their intention was practical or ritualistic. Having regressed to a neoprimitive state, they didn't make such distinctions. The tallest member of the crowd, possibly an albino, collected the golf clubs, replaced them into a red, white, and blue bag, and took out a small firearm. He shot the vending machine point blank before leading his tribe away in silence.

A smell that I initially mistook for a burning plastic revealed itself to be roasting corn, as I came upon a radiant young woman hunched over a camp stove onto which she was tamping down tortilla dough. I watched her deftly flip and stack the perfectly browned cakes as flames licked the side of the stove, which she occasionally nudged with the toe of her boot. She reminded me of an eighty-year-old peasant in a documentary about a cyclone-swept land. She had that unhurried efficiency, that lack of theatricality. Nevertheless, I knew she knew I was standing there.

Even in this light, I could tell that her eyes were violet. We exchanged no words, but I understood I was to follow as she joined three others on a sloping cement pylon that must have once anchored a bridge that spanned the river here. A few empty lemonade cans were littered about, and as I approached, a gust toppled one and sent it half-rolling, half-sliding into the water. We watched as the current heaved it westward.

I couldn't tell whether my presence was nonchalantly tolerated or had forced them to postpone subversive planning. The latter didn't strike me as all that likely: these weren't terrorists, more like carefree pranksters indulging in guerilla theatrics for their own sake. They might just as easily have been protesting media monopolies or exorbitant tuition or, for that matter, the scarcity of gourmet ice cream or the injustice of having been born in the twenty-first century.

A tall, dirty protestor in a rather modish lavender anorak rose to deliver a sarcasm-scarred rendition of an open letter from Drixa that had run in the *Tribune* that evening:

What Are the Facts about H_2O?
We can't claim with 100% certainty that H_2O = water, but to the best of our knowledge no method exists to tell one apart from the other. In independent labs, pure water and samples of our product have been subjected to a rigorous battery of state-of-the-art identification technologies, and not a single difference [*a crooked index finger jabbed at the sky*] has emerged. Rumors abound of "sensitives" who can identify H_2O with one sip, but so such feat has yet been demonstrated to our satisfaction.

Therefore, we confidently [*the finger went comically limp*] recommend H_2O for ALL of your household water uses and just as confidently refute all claims of side effects. Fear of the new is a natural human reaction, but to persist in such fears despite an overwhelming body of reassuring evidence is simply irrational and, at this point in history, reckless to the point of suicidal. [*the jagged nail leaving a pink line where the jugular was presumed to be.*]

The performance received a polite round of applause and low whistles meant to evoke a stadium of rabid fans. Aqua snatched the paper from the reader's hands, folded it into a boat, and sent it downstream.

"Caution is cowardice," she said. "Debate is dangerous, right? No matter how many times technology betrays us, it would be reckless not to trust it."

"What other choice do we have?" I asked.

"That's the one I hate," she said. "All you scalpel-happy surgeons pretending to want to save the patient. Second opinions? Questions? Sign this waiver and let us cut you open. Then we'll talk."

"I'm here, Aqua. What questions do you have?" I said, hoping they wouldn't be too hard.

The water barely seeped by, pearlescent and brilliant green. There was no reflection, just the roiled green foam of leaked by-products and one-celled life forms. Two spotted carp swam by in the murk. It looked like one was carrying the other, a groom and bride, but the bride was dead. Upon further inspection, I saw they shared a spine.

"Did Lionel send you?"

"I think Warne Shoals did."

"Did you invent H_2O?"

"That's what it looks like."

"Do you feel personally responsible for it?"

"If it's a Drixa product, then it's their responsibility. Personally? I do see where you're coming from."

"Are you going to sign the Letter of Agreement, Hayden?"

"These are difficult questions."

"They're yes or no."

"Those are the hardest kind."

The protestor who had read the Drixa letter pointed to me. "This guy does Lionel Dawson better than anybody," he said, rolling a leaflet into a cylinder and brandishing it like a microphone. I recognized that refusal was not an option.

You're credited with the salvation of pure drinking water

for close to a billion people, and yet there are some critics out there who say you've exploited a global crisis and excluded billions more by holding onto the patent for your filtration technology. How do you respond to these charges?

I give you my word that Drixa is not standing by idly while any community, anywhere on the planet lacks pure drinking water. We fund a program for installing and maintaining more than ten thousand free filters around the globe, each of them powerful enough to deliver clean water to ten thousand people.

Those efforts are commendable, no doubt, but wouldn't it be more effective to release the specifications for your filters so that rather than awaiting Drixa's beneficence, communities could build their own?

We think it would be irresponsible to open that door to imitators not guaranteed to implement the quality control we practice, whether it's due to fecklessness or it's well-intentioned imprecision. Drixa technology demands stewardship and expertise found exclusively in our network of licensed installers.

So why not train and license more installers? Lives are at stake!

That's why we're going as fast as we can and no faster, because lives are at stake.

This was truly one of my best performances: The answers issued from me spontaneously and with the vocabulary, cadence, and register of my boss's boss's boss, but before the applause could swell, something crashed behind us, and a silhouetted albino

64

climbed out of a dumpster, dragging wet cardboard and a hulking piece of unidentifiable debris. The crashing continued, gradually resolving into a thunderous rhythm that gave me the feeling of hostile forces driving us into the fetid river.

Aqua sprang up and skipped toward the dumpster.

"Should we go after her?" I asked, though I sensed already that the question was off the mark.

"I'd rather go after *him*," the tall protestor chuckled.

I turned to go.

"Hey," he said. "Where did H_2O come from?"

"Drixa's commitment to innovation lies deep within its DNA. We have a firm belief in actualizing potential. That's a good place to start, if you want to look."

"Thank you, Lionel Dawson," he said. "But I was speaking to Hayden Shivers. Where did you get the idea for H_2O? It's evil, man, but it's sort of marvelous, too. I mean, it's like a bottomless glass."

"Ever been to Malta?" I asked, realizing that my answer could turn out to be the rough draft for the legend and trying to imagine how Lionel would tell it. What belonged in and what belonged out?

CHAPTER EIGHT

When we decided on a honeymoon destination, neither Ginelle nor I knew how dramatically this choice would affect the rest of our lives, each in our own way. And of course by the time Malta was through with us, we didn't belong together anymore. Some honeymoon.

I certainly never set out to solve the hydrocrisis. In fact, the whole point was to take my mind off work for a few weeks. A big drain project had missed a crucial deadline, and I'd been putting in so much overtime in the weeks before the wedding that I often dreamed in the language of plumbing.

The ceremony was entirely pleasant, perhaps lacking in thrills, and the flights from Chicago to Rome and Rome to Malta were uneventful. We weren't eager to spend time in our cramped hotel room, so, dazed and bleary, we booked an afternoon cruise on a yacht called (what else?) the Maltese Falcon. The Philippine crew came around with Italian grappa and Moroccan sausages. Too shy to ask somebody to take our picture, Ginelle and I took pictures of each other.

"What's that?" another passenger asked, pointing to a mound jutting from the sea.

"It is called Fungus Rock." The Cornish skipper said that the Crusaders had rubbed the fungus over the tips of their divining rods to help them find drinking water in the desert. Like most sailors, this one was full of stories. He even dropped anchor so we could lean over the railing and look down at what was once the Continent of Atlantis.

"One member of the crew would collect the fungus in burlap sacks before departing on lengthy or hazardous journeys. If supplies of drinking water ran low, the fungus would be used to sweeten the seawater."

"A desalinization agent," I murmured.

"Yes," he said.

"But how?" I asked.

"Sailors have their secrets."

"And their legends," rejoined the passenger.

The next morning, I woke before Ginelle and bought her a seed pearl necklace at the first market stall that I found open. The gift made her more suspicious than grateful, but she didn't protest when I set out alone for the docks, where a sailboat could be chartered. At the foot of Fungus Rock, I came across a bearded German making an orange-pink paste with a large mortar and pestle, oblivious to the surf crashing all around him.

"What do you want with the fungus?" I asked, already feeling proprietary.

"It isn't fungus, it's plant," he said, holding a pinch up to the light, as if that proved something. "It has evolved a unique survival mechanism to cope with sporadic droughts."

"What do you care?"

"I'm a biologist, I care."

"It knows there's a drought."

"Cells don't know anything. It stores water in its fibers for long periods and releases it when the need develops."

"Like a cactus."

"Yes, but unlike a cactus, a sort of subatomic switcheroo takes place. It's quite hard to document because each sample behaves differently, depending on circumstances that may be too subtle for to measure."

"What, like alchemy?"

"No," he said, amused by my choice of such a majestic word. Say an ounce of this paste absorbs a liquid ounce of water.

Altogether it weighs how much, would you think?"

"Not two ounces?"

"We've measured as much as two point oh nine. The harsher the drought, the more sudden, the more the samples weigh."

For some reason, I just had to get my hands on it, to feel it between my fingers. "And what do you get out of the deal?" I asked, elbowing the man aside so I could get to the stuff.

"If I get two point one, an editor at *Science* says he'll let me write it up."

This remark baffled me, and then it enraged me. I don't know where my anger came from, but it came all in a rush, like an oilrig spewing its first black gush: "Don't tell me you don't see the applications. Think about the acres you could irrigate. The death and disease you could eradicate. Think what you've done, my God, to desert warfare. Soldiers fighting on and on without having to so much as stop to refill their canteens, because of course you could just graft this stuff into their kidneys to make every man his own water fountain." The thing was, if you'd given me a pad and paper at that moment I could have sketched out each of these applications.

Perhaps it was the Mediterranean sun roasting my brain, or maybe inhaling the salt air—or the fungus itself—was doing something to me. My only sense was of falling, but not with my body, with my language: the words tumbled out, and the only way to catch them was to slow the rant down, pulling back against it firmly without yanking. "And that's why . . . you may want . . . to . . . to publish your findings . . . without any . . . delay."

I was a man possessed by an idea that I could not communicate, as was clear from the researcher's response. "Yes," my audience of one said, hurriedly packing his supplies. "All very interesting." Nor did I myself quite understand the idea, if you could call it that, for if I had, you can bet it would have been subject to a quick and painless abortion.

With her groom off on this errand, Ginelle walked around the it-Toqq on Rabat, where three different women insisted that she had her mother's face. Mother? She'd never known hers and brushed the remarks off with a joke about the beauty of Maltese women.

The noise of the market, the color of the stones, the slant of the sun all felt familiar to her. She kept catching glimpses of faces of the people she thought she knew, before realizing, of course, she knew nobody here. The scent of peas baked in a pastry made her day-dream in a language she didn't understand.

Ginelle grew up in Chicago but had never felt at home there. She found Chicagoans too direct, and at the same time too ready to talk about nothing. She felt both rushed and impatient. Loyal, though not profoundly attached, to her adopted mother and father, she had never had any curiosity about her birth parents, but over time, and especially during a difficult pregnancy and whenever she saw her son's face in a certain light, she became convinced that the gaps in her adoption papers might be filled here, on this forgotten archipelago concealed by Sicily. The prospect of a Maltese identity, absurd at first, had become something she would believe until it was disproved.

I believe that Malta itself filled a need of Ginelle's, became her motherland, restored a missing chromosome, and let her join a struggle she could call her own, but it was by no means easy coming home so late in life. She told herself it was for Hayden Jr.'s sake: she loved the kid so much she had to find out where he came from, even if it meant leaving him behind.

And when she did, she left me with a card bearing the phone number to the Snowflake Lodge.

"Dr. Hayden Shivers?"

"This is he, but I'm not a—"

"This is Mr. Varuk Prechand. Your wife call about a . . . 'maid,' no?"

"Yes, Ginelle will be on Malta for six weeks and I need someone to take over the household chores, but I'm very particular. Are your maids careful about their personal behavior and appearance?"

"Yes, Doctor Shivers? We have much beautiful maids."

"Well, beautiful."

"You don't want maid with wart or bad-smelling breath or big ankle. She never make the bed, she wash white underwears with new red towel, but she got pretty face and laughing to your jokes, no?"

"I didn't say that."

Prechand cleared his throat. "It's okay, Doctor Shivers. I fax you pictures, you pick maid with . . . skills you are requiring."

"I just don't want to pick wrong. I think of a maid as a partner. We have, or I have a young son. Did I mention that?"

"I do not have wrong girls. Take one. If she is 'wrong,' you send her back within a week for full refund. After a week, the cash is gone, but it is okay to . . . exchange your maid for another."

"How many . . . "

"Three. Three girls, three weeks, but remember, you send back two and you get a third, and she is still the wrong girl, the first two are not happily coming back to you."

I called the Snowflake Lodge back to ask for more pictures. The voice on the other end was amused.

"What do you do, Doctor Shivers?"

"I'm an engineer with Drixa."

"Yes," Prechand said. "I know Drixa."

"I also work independently in the basement of my home," I heard myself elaborating. The scramble for water had given scientists credibility they hadn't enjoyed since the dawn of the nuclear age. Every inventor, chemistry Ph.D., and home alchemist was provided with funding and equipment on the barest of pretexts. The press announced and discredited breakthroughs on a weekly basis.

"And your field is what?"

"Ah, it's kind of hard to say at this point. Do you know anything about physics?"

"I'm looking out for my girls. What kind of environment is the home? What is the nature of the work conducted down in the basement? Put it in general terms, if you would."

"This is how I like to think of it. Stop me if you're getting bored."

"Not at all."

"It's a slightly different approach to the water crisis. Perhaps you've read of the recent discoveries about molecules. Some molecules lead a dual existence, like a melody that fits in two compositions, one written a hundred years after the other." I wanted to say more but knew enough to be vague. This could be anybody on the line. Every day, corporations, governments, and the media burned new espionage channels in pursuit of moisture.

"You are building water machine."

"It's not a machine. I don't think I should say any more about it."

"Such exciting area for Dr. Shivers to research. Man of science, he needing support of good a woman. How unfortunate, Missus Shivers going to Yalta without you."

"Malta. She's searching for her birth mother."

"Yes, how unfortunate. I know somebody, who will be loyal and . . . supportive. To help you make your science projects and to keep clean house. Dr. Shivers, maybe someday I come to Chicago and see water machine. Science it's a . . . hobby of myself, too."

"It's not a machine."

"So then what?"

Better not to answer that one. I had had a kind of breakthrough of my own, an astonishing gush of real water from a source not determined. I'd rigged a filter from the handle of an old electric toothbrush, a modulator, the loop of a magnifying glass with the lens pushed out, and, stretched over that, a drumhead of mosquito netting. A thin paste of crushed Maltese fungus coated the netting. But it was no time to celebrate. The next time I tried it, the result had practically vanished. Some things happen only once.

"What I'd like most right now is to fail, to come to an impasse. Then I could tell myself I had responsibly followed a ghost trail, closed it off in the name of science, leaving a signpost up for future investigators that says NOT A THROUGH STREET. Instead, every new experiment seems to confirm a set of physical laws not yet recorded."

"What about black girl? The sweet black girl of Africa, okay?"

Chapter Nine

It doesn't happen often, but sometimes at the movies the projectionist will accidentally thread the wrong reel. We're sitting in the dark, happily watching a girl in medieval garb riding bareback through the woods, whipping the beast between her legs to go faster so that she might reach the castle in time to warn her brothers about the impostor priest, when abruptly the scene shifts to a game of dominoes at a folding table on the street in Cairo. There's a moment of silent incomprehension and then our voices rise as one in a bloodthirsty plea to give us back the heroine's desperate ride.

ICE-9 alleged that H_2O could produce similar effects on the brain. Inarguably, something had gone wrong, events had slipped out of position, and yet nobody around me appeared to notice. What could I do but assume I'd missed a beat and proceed as if one moment followed the next as a drop of water follows another from a leaky faucet?

Miyumi found me chatting with the ICE-9 protestors and yanked me back into the car, and we waded through the dense nighttime traffic that ringed the city. Our destination was not identified, but I could tell it wasn't the same as the day before. We headed past the turn for my drains and onto a northbound highway I'd never taken.

Looking concerned, she produced a can of Country Life Lemonade and held it to my forehead. Instead of relief, the aluminum evoked a lesson from high school physics: the cold object (can) didn't imbue the warm object (head) with coolness; it drew energy or therms away from it. The feeling that the warm object was being cooled was not to be trusted. This seemed germane.

"No thanks," I said hoarsely. "I'm not thirsty."

"If you don't drink it I will."

"Then drink it," I dared her. The darkness made it hard to grasp where we were headed.

"Anyway, I've got my own can," she said.

"Drink from this one." I stared at her with a mindless determination that she should have recognized as Harrison Fordian.

She raised an eyebrow. "What do you think this is?"

With matters of trust, it all depends on what you sniff out of a situation, and I smelled something rotten. "Let's trade cans," I proposed. "You drink from this one, and I'll drink from that one."

She assumed a baffled look, momentarily embarrassing me, before saying, "Hallelujah," taking the can, popping the tab, and drinking half down. She wiped her mouth with her sleeve triumphantly. Then she made that aah sound some people make after drinking something cold. Shrugging, I popped her tab and took a sheepish sip. First I felt nothing. Then a wave of good will washed over me, the sense of being well cared for, even coddled.

Organizations had replaced God, and maybe the family as well. Rewards were infinite, but punishments could be severe. Lemonade had replaced water, and the sweeteners and souring agents posed a greater threat than the pollutants they masked. (The most popular brand, Country Life, was manufactured by the Committee of Lifelong Access, which invariably blamed Drixa for the poor quality of the water it supplied. Drixa, of course, asserted that it was impossible to filter out certain flavor additives once they found their way into the water table.)

Moisture left our bodies as fast as we could replace it. The future replaced the past every instant. Everything was replaceable, but that didn't mean anything was equivalent. When Ginelle left for Malta, I had replaced her, hadn't I? As the car moved through neighborhoods I had never seen before, my heart swam in a lemonade bath, and I smiled murkily, suppressing a spasm at the base of my spine.

We came upon a few trailers in an empty lot ringed by forest. Beside one trailer there was another vehicle with a steel arm holding aloft a basket large enough for one man. The word for such a vehicle escaped me. The man was Lionel Dawson.

Miyumi handed me a brochure as I asked, "What's this?"—meaning the set-up.

"Inspiration," she said.

H_2O = water
a tall, cool one
the cold glass sweats
ice cubes pop
a drop rolls down your chin
and into your shirt
impossible to stop
making that ah sound
—jason f., hope ridge

drink up, boys
houseplants thrive
with a daily misting.
that's for the leaves
the roots need care, too
not too little, not too much
not by the radiator
—ladonna m., berkeley

hot drinks in January
cider, tea, coffee
mulled wine, glug,
water with lemon,
hot chocolate with
marshmallows and a
cinnamon stick
—keith b., lincoln

My lips moved as I read. Soon, I found myself inside one of the trailers. Out the window, behemoth cameras and heavy equipment aimed at a frail boy seated at a picnic table lighted to look like mid-afternoon, though it was still the dead of night. Flanked by fake trees sat Hayden Jr.

I leaned forward to get a better view of my son, but concentration was difficult, and my attention kept returning to the brochure, which was on a pillow, which was on my lap. Keith B.? Ladonna? What were they trying to tell me? Were they participants in the marketing campaign or hostages to it? Someone was issuing commands in echoey, dull tones that had to do with the speaker using one of those cones that projects the voice. "Fill the glass a little higher. Higher, higher. Okay! Now, kid, you've gone above and beyond, and we all appreciate it. Now what we're asking is that you go *above and beyond* above and beyond."

Hayden Jr. said something plaintive, the meaning of which I could not quite divine. Somebody replied, "That's just great, Hay. Pretend there's a gold coin at the bottom of the glass. We're going to get started in just a minute, so hold that thought in your head." There was another, gruffer voice. Then the person with the cone announced, "Somebody, powder his face. Steve's getting too much shine."

I would have liked to call out to Hayden Jr., but at the moment I was once again absorbed in the brochure. Would Ladonna and Keith come forward when this was all done and admit that they knowingly gave false testimonials?

Lionel yelled, "Action." Even through the cone, he sounded somewhat presidential. (*Megaphone*. The word came to me like a mosquito bite.) I raised myself to the window in time to watch my son reaching for the glass. But his little hand didn't move accurately, and his knuckles grazed the side. The glass didn't overturn, but some droplets splashed out. When the boy started to bring his wet knuckles to his lips, an assistant sprang from the sidelines and yanked him by the wrist.

"Not water, not water," the assistant wailed. Unfazed, Hayden Jr. righted himself and beamed. "It's H_2O," he said, as if it was a line he'd rehearsed.

"No, no, no, no, no. This is a commercial for Drixa H_2O, but the liquid in the glass is just a special effect, remember? Don't you know what *nonpotable* means?"

The boy thought the whole thing was deliriously funny. "I wasn't going to really drink it. Don't you know what *acting* means?"

I had tucked the pillow under my arm and stepped out of the trailer just when the phone rang, the phone in the suede bag at the foot of the machine in which Lionel sat. The name of this vehicle escaped me. "Dawson here," I said into the mouthpiece.

"I'm glad it's you," the reporter said. His voice trembled, but he was obviously emboldened by the occasion. "I'd like to play you a recording and get your comment."

"Shoot," I said.

There were three voices on the tape. Lionel, Miyumi, and Mayor King. There were some preliminary niceties, and then the mayor asked, "Is there enough water?"

"That's the decision we're asking you to make," Lionel replied. "What about the vibrations? Wasn't all that racket supposed to solve our problem?"

Miyumi cleared her throat. "As you know, the facility has ben-efited the people of Chicago in significant and measurable ways."

"Don't do that. We don't have enough time for that."

"Yet in this particular instance," she continued, "an alternative solution is the one we're proposing. When conventional filtration falls short, there are options. In situations such as this."

"This what?" the mayor said. "This *crisis*?"

"I wouldn't presume," she said.

"If it's not a crisis, what am I doing here at four in the morning?" the mayor said. "If you're telling me there's something in the water, that's your problem. If you're telling me there's something in the water that you can't filter out, that's my crisis."

Lionel spoke up, "If it never happens, it's no crisis."

"Do I want to hear this?"

"We have a general perception that a new, waterlike substance is in circulation. At the moment, that perception is erroneous, but it's useful to us in that it serves as a gauge of public sentiment."

Miyumi read aloud from a file: "Widespread apathy. A fringe is concerned. A fringe of that fringe is actively concerned, asking questions, taking precautions."

Lionel sneered, "The transition will be smooth. A ten-minute interruption of service, maximum, while the new water main is activated. A brief and touching ceremony."

And then Lionel said my name. In fact, he had been calling over and over again, but at first the voice hadn't registered as originating from a source other than the phone. "Hayden, you're needed on the set. Hayden Shivers, Senior, is needed on the set."

Warne Shoals said, "Hello, hello?"

I spoke into the phone, using phrases I knew Lionel would use, though maybe not in this context: "Shoals, you've done good work. You're a fine reporter. You've gone above and beyond."

"Can I quote you on that?"

"No," I said. "You cannot," and dropped the phone back in Lionel's bag. Most of the cameras and equipment were gone, but the Director was still high in the cherry picker. He looked down and said, "Hey, pal. You look great. I'm going to give the make-up guy a raise. Let's get to work."

"Thanks."

"And Hayden Jr. What a sharp boy. He handled the shoot like a pro, just like you said he would."

"Thank you." The strain of looking upwards made me feel dazed again.

"You're welcome. Now let's get to work so we can get out of here and get to where we want to be. I see you brought a pillow with you."

"What, *this*?"

"It's fine for rehearsal. We don't want to bruise you up and down before tomorrow."

One assistant brought over a stool of varnished wood, and another handed me some water in a cheap glass. "Is this okay to drink?" I asked.

"Is that supposed to be a joke?" The assistant looked as though he'd kill himself if someone cracked just one more joke.

Lionel called through the megaphone to clear the set, but first Miyumi ran up to me. "Purple doesn't say victim."

"This is heather."

"Who?"

A third assistant came running with a powder-blue shirt still warm from the iron. While changing, I caught a whiff of something sweet and putrid, as if my sweat glands were emitting toxins, but the shirt was a perfect fit. I placed the pillow on the ground next to the stool.

"Whenever you're ready," Lionel megaphoned. "Let's see you die." We locked stares for a moment, exchanging permission for what was about to happen. If my eyes betrayed uncertainty, Lionel's didn't acknowledge it.

The word raced around my mind. *Die* had many possible meanings. Performing badly in public was known as flopping or dying. Unbearable anticipation, as in *dying to see you again*. Falling in love, or, more specifically, reaching orgasm, was *dying*, too. This meaning was antiquated, but it had been revived in a recent pop song: *Could I die in your arms tonight*. Of course there was dying of shame, of embarrassment, or heartbreak or jealousy. And then there was the simple and unmetaphorical variety, the only one that made unmistakable sense in this context. A thousand movie death scenes riddled my heart.

> *gunshot from a jealous husband waiting in the backseat of a parked car*
> *rich old man dying in bed, surrounded by all his ex-wives*
> *convertible rolling backwards off a cliff*
> *drunk teenager electrocuted during an icestorm*

Given the circumstances, I realized I shouldn't have been surprised—and upon further consideration, I considered it to have been perfectly logical—that this word was spoken aloud. Still, for whatever reason I hadn't been prepared, and the word *die* struck me in the sternum. My heart felt inflamed under my shirt, my throat coated with ash.

> *bullet in the back while crawling under the prison wall*
> *bullet in the neck while sinking into the tub*
> *bullet piercing the torsos of two kids slow-dancing at prom*
> *police car slamming into a wall of oil barrels*
> *fat cop tripping over the gutter atop high rise*

Balancing the water, I climbed up on the stool. My boy was watching. The Director clearly expected me to know the script. Miyumi pantomimed something. She took a sip from an invisible cup and then put her hands together and took an exaggerated bow. At first I thought it was some kind of prayer. For me? Then I understood she was miming. I nodded, lifted the glass to my lips, counted silently to myself—one Mississippi, two Mississippi—and then dove off the stool, catching the corner of the pillow with my shoulder. A large man with a broom appeared to sweep up the glass.

I lay flat, feeling pretty good about the whole motion of the fall, though I knew that it was too deliberate and that my landing lacked grace. I hadn't been able to keep from bracing myself. Lionel would have noticed.

"One more time. Get him another," the director announced. I mounted the stool again and repeated the fall. This time instead of diving I slumped, but too slowly, and the glass didn't break when it hit the ground. The next time, the glass broke, but I was grimacing on the way down, anticipating the force of impact. Lionel reminded me to let my body go limp, to keep my eyes and mouth open, not to make any sound upon landing. The *oof* makes it unrealistic, he said. Let the earth itself knock the wind out of you.

It came down to three steps: concentration, then relaxation, then gravitation. Finally, I got the fall exactly right. I concentrated, counting one mississippi, two mississippi and relaxed every muscle as I slid off the stool, letting gravity pull me down. The glass shattered. I nailed the pillow and bounced slightly.

The whole set (maybe six people total) burst into applause. Lionel pronounced it a remarkable fall. I sprang up and took in the adulation. It was especially gratifying to have executed such a remarkable fall while Hayden Jr. looked on.

The boy applauded longer than anybody else. Then he was holding his stomach and rocking with laughter. I was thrilled to be entertaining my son like this, now that it was becoming apparent how little chance there was of that we would sustain a normal father-son relationship. If Hayden Jr. wouldn't be seeing his father very often from then on, at least the impression left in his mind would be of an unlikely clown. That was an important lesson to pass along, wasn't it? In a world pushed to the edge of catastrophe, there was still grace in a pratfall.

The director kept making me repeat the fall from the stool, to make my muscles memorize it. It's easy to fall, but not so easy to fall *just right*. One or two of those falls during rehearsal I'd put alongside the finest accomplishments of my life. When it was over, great joy overcame great exhaustion, followed by feeble delirium that instantly lifted when I looked over again at Hayden Jr.'s tensed shoulders. He wasn't laughing after all, but trembling with unrecognizable emotion, icewater tears leaking off his eyelashes. I brushed myself off and limped over to him. "It's okay, Hay, it's okay," I said. Would embracing the boy reassure or alarm him? The hug that resulted from this deliberation was tentative and forced. What kind of man doesn't know how to hug his boy, his own boy? "Nothing happened to me. I was only pretending to fall. I mean, I really did fall, of course, all of those times, over and over, and I won't say it didn't hurt at all, but . . . look. It was all on purpose, so you don't have to worry."

"It's not that, Dad, it's just that I like lemonade. Water tastes funny."

"Come on, let me put you in a car. Pierre will take you home," I said.

"I want you to take me."

"Of course," I said. "I'll come for the ride, but we can't let your mom think it was my idea for you to come out here."

"What about Yemina?"

"She left, Hay, remember? She took very good care of us while your mother was away, and then she had to go."

"Nuh-uh."

"Uh-huh."

"Oh yeah," he said. "I keep forgetting what I'm supposed to forget."

"What does that mean?"

"I dunno."

"It's okay, never mind."

Chapter Ten

Kenwood was one of Chicago's nicer neighborhoods, with clean streets and a courteous but deadly security force. On Kenwood Avenue, east of South Forty-Eighth Street, low shrubs surrounded a two-story home painted yellow whose most distinct feature was a portico supported by eight ionic pillars.

My son let me into the house that I once called mine. Except for one thing, the interior had remained the same. The sofa set, desk set, and stereo set retained their positions on the green-gold carpeting, and there were even wedding pictures up. Probably Ginelle kept them so as not to disturb Hayden Jr., or else she simply hadn't noticed.

But, yes, there was one difference: replacing a poster of O'Keeffe's *Sky above Clouds*, an eight-foot-wide red-and-white flag hung above the sofa. It was a banner of pride and protest, the exact opposite of the painting insofar as images can have opposites. The horizontal composition, with fluffy white supporting pure blue, invited contemplation and, more important, imagination, whereas the vertical orientation of the flag enforced inviolable borders—red on the right, white on the left. Ginelle's Maltese identity had intensified. Ignored and exploited at Europe's convenience, Malta had endured wave upon wave of pirates, crusaders, and profiteers for thirty or more centuries. Ginelle harbored a searing resentment for empires and emperors, Napoleon above all. The more she read about the quiet piety of Malta's inhabitants, the more she despised the flashy, self-satisfied hauteur of the empire that had sprung up lately on the banks of Lake Michigan.

Aside from celebrating Malta, she was defending its right to be left alone, not isolated from the world, but not dominated by it either. Was that so much to ask for? When she put it to me, the question didn't sound rhetorical, and I found myself stammering out a defense of humankind's civilizing impulse, sounding like an apologist for history's endless roster of conquerors.

Two pearl-gray ballet slippers were on two different steps leading up to the bedroom. Invitation? Accusation?

Ginelle never found her mother; the tip she'd received turned out to be bogus after two frustrating, enervating months in Maltese limbo. She lost twenty pounds and developed a severe pain between her shoulders that made it hard for her to lift Hayden Jr. I poured on the concern, becoming an adept drier of meat, creating sophisticated and subtle jerkies of chicken, salmon, and venison. The dehydrator was a engineering marvel, an aerodynamic and responsive instrument. I never stopped to wonder how it had entered our home.

And then there was sex. By varying the intensity and pitch of vibration on the device adapted from my work in the basement, then by passing one wavelength over another, I prolonged and enriched the experience. A keyboard capable of spinning subtle fractal symphonies replaced the high-low switch of a modified wand. Ginelle looked at me one way in bed—a luxuriant, animal hunger—and another way everywhere else. Recognizing that I'd become obsolete again if she ever learned to do for herself what I did for her, I ensured that the modulator linking wand and keyboard stayed hidden.

"Hayden, how is your research going? I'd say it's going very well."

"I need more time to fit all the variables into a coherent system."

"Oh, silly, you're brilliant. And the house is in much better shape than I expected. That maid was worth the money. What was her name again?"

"Yemina."

"Right, Yemina from Gambia."

"Zambia," I corrected, wishing I hadn't.

"Of course. Anyway, Hayden Jr. seems to have liked her. It's too bad she couldn't stay on."

On the refrigerator: photographs of a family trip to a tropical rainforest; of Ginelle and I on our Maltese honeymoon; and of Ginelle alone on Malta, some years later, with a headache squint. (Who took that picture? And why put it up?)

Something in the freezer gave me a start. I shut the door before it could lodge in my memory.

"Would you like some Country Life?"

"No, I'll get it. I remember where it is."

Ginelle stood in the doorway, her complexion gone waxy, her practical bob frizzed out like an August dandelion. She seemed annoyed, but then she almost always seemed annoyed. She didn't seem *especially* annoyed by either her son's nighttime excursion, if she knew about it, or by my presence in the house she'd unmistakably asked me to leave.

She fingered her bare throat, and in a tone that suggested she'd already explained once, she said, "Hayden Jr. says he wants to become a scientist."

"It's one way to make a difference in the world," I said. Were there really fish sticks in the freezer? I was picturing two stacks of fish stick boxes, one stack of six "with baked-in cocktail sauce flavor" and another stack of four "with baked-in tartar sauce flavor," but it was conceivable that I hadn't even opened the freezer during this visit and was thinking of another time. That smell, that melted wax smell that a fish would never recognize, hanging in the air could be a trick played by my imagination.

"He has that kind of mind."

"Of course," I said. "There are good differences and bad differences. How it's applied, and where, that's what counts."

"I suppose that's true." She wouldn't meet my gaze, but her

87

very aversion seemed to beg me, the husband she held in contempt, to beg me for forgiveness or at least understanding. Or maybe she just wanted me to go.

As I let myself out, a voice called my name from the bushes.

"Julian?" I said. "Want to come up here and tell me what's going on?"

He shook his head, indicating his intention to remain there in the shrubbery. On my behalf, of course. He waved some letters, and I joined him in the shadow of an overgrown hedge, where he leaned against a pillar.

"What are you even doing here?"

"The Snowflake Lodge. Urgent request," he read.

I took the letter from him, but he pawed at my forearm to gain a view, and we read together.

Dear Shivers?
Where the girl?
Were waiting for her to telephone already two week. This information must be telephoned 312-568-28340 before it is any more to long. When the information is telephoned by only the girl will be permission to extend the contract.

"It doesn't really say anything," I said, hopefully. "There's no accusation, no implication. It's just a form letter."

"Right, just an overdue notice. I would ignore it." He started to tuck it into his jacket, but I bent back two of his stout fingers and snatched it back.

The Snowflake Lodge had a reputation as one of the more humane agencies of its kind, but that was a relative claim in this business, and it would stretch the meaning of the word to describe Yemina's experience with them as lucky.

"You going to call?" he asked, twisting a spiny branch in his hands.

"Your counsel would be welcomed here."

"Let me ask you this. Is there information?"

"Not at this time."

"No information, no call."

I appreciated the brevity of the argument. What would I tell them? That I went down to the basement to look for her and found two feet of crystalline water? And then I simply gave up?

Of course, my first thought had been the sump pump, but Yemina was too good a plumber to botch that. I had managed to drain the basement and sweep out every trace of her, every box of fishsticks, and kitchenware catalogue, but life never did return to normal. Enlisting Hayden Jr. in the cleanup effort—probably not the most sensitive parental act in history. But he hadn't seemed to mind keeping "our secret from Mom." It had made him feel grown-up, which come to think of it does have a positive influence on a child his age.

—Where are her shoes?

—I dunno, maybe she was wearing them.

—Is that all she had, one pair?

—Uh-huh, I think so . . . oh, whoops, here they are.

—Good boy. Now what did she sleep in?

—I dunno. Do you?

—What does that mean?

—I dunno.

—It's okay, forget it.

For Julian, three years of law school could be boiled down to two words: admit nothing. He probably got more out of his legal education than most. "Are you going back to the Justice Complex?" I asked.

"Las Vegas," he replied. "I've got this funny feeling."

CHAPTER ELEVEN

I wished I'd used the bathroom before leaving the house. The sweat on my face and neck stung my skin when the wind blew, and my bladder winced, but at least the hotel was nearby. I looked around for landmarks to establish my position on the way home. Neither the row of high trees to my right nor the street sign ahead, coming into focus to read Whitman, meant anything.

A large billboard sent a tremor of anxiety through me. It took a minute to register as vandalism.

The *Tribune* would call it Drixa's first public relations blunder. Nobody would blame the perpetrators, whose exploitation of such opportunities, rare as they were, had come to be understood.

A well-placed dash of black electrical tape turned $=$ into $\neq$, transforming reassurance into alarm. A thousand of these diagonal lines tilted the city anew, and you could feel something wrong in the air.

A bolt of exasperation hit me, along with an involuntary clench in the kidneys. I would have to find somewhere to relieve myself before I could get my bearings. Right now, I felt lower than a dog— even dogs could go in the street.

At the corner of Berkeley and Forty-fifth, the lights were on in a masonry row house with a white-stone driveway. A bright-eyed plastic deer stood guard on the lawn; I gave it a head fake and raced up to the door.

"Hello there, this is embarrassing, but I'm a little lost and I need to use—"

"—the phone?" A big-boned hausfrau stood in the doorway, arms akimbo and jaw square.

"Just to use—"

"—a compass?" she offered.

"My name's Hayden Shivers."

"You said you were lost." Mrs. Deer peered at me, and she stepped back to permit my entry, thinking maybe I recognized her or vice versa. Laughter (hers amused, mine anxious) filled the hallway en route to the guest bathroom. The walls were striped blue and blue-green. The toilet seat was already up, indicating the existence of a Mr. Deer. For some reason, the blow dryer was turned on, and I toggled it off to help me relax.

The piss felt great, and I stood there inhaling and exhaling, trying to make my muscles slacken. A film of sweat glazed my face. I raised my arms over my head, wiggled my fingers, and opened my mouth as wide as it would go. The piss kept coming out of me, a steady stream that showed no sign of tapering.

Was somebody listening at the door? And would they wonder at this endless stream, this waterfall maintaining its intensity after—what?—forty, fifty seconds. Was there a possibility that I had ingested a small amount of Maltese fungus and inadvertently turned my body into a fountain? Or was this a message from ICE-9, a warning about the perils of H_2O? It made me wonder how ICE-9 could possibly have gained control of my bladder.

After a worrisome instant when the piss actually intensified, it finally became a trickle and then a few stubborn drops before shutting off altogether. I stood there for a few more seconds to make sure it was really over.

The soap was still in its wrapper, and I hesitated to use it until realizing that not washing would look much worse than spoiling a new bar of soap. The water streaming from the faucet had a thin, lacy texture, a bit off. I wondered whether this was one of the communities Drixa was testing H_2O on. Another possibility: this was actual water and the stuff at the Brahms Hotel wasn't.

Every light in the house was on and all the appliances running. The vacuum cleaner stood in the middle of the room, quivering with the effort of sucking at the same spot. A blender chopped air molecules while the dishwasher ran hollowly. On television, the announcer declared that history was in the making. Mr. and Mrs. Deer sat in front of a large TV set, sharing a bowl of chips. For a while I obligingly waited in the electricity-draining hum.

"WHY IS EVERYTHING ON?"

"WE'RE RUNNING THE POWER."

"THAT'S WHAT I SAID."

"CAN I TURN THIS OFF?" I said, reaching for a portable radio on high static.

"WE'RE SUPPOSED TO RUN THE POWER FOR NINETY MINUTES BEFORE PLUGGING IN THE WATER FILTER, TO PREVENT BLINKS AND SURGES."

"WE HAD TO GET A FILTER FOR THE WATER."

"THE H_2O." I tried not to sound defensive.

"EXACTLY," Mrs. Deer said. "WE'RE SUPPOSED TO RUN THE POWER BEFORE WE HOOK UP THE FILTER, OR ELSE IT CHOKES ON THE WATER." She touched the ends of her hair with her fingers, ready to pull out a hank. They held a brief, stage-whisper huddle I could hear every world of.

"WHO'S THAT?'

"I DON'T KNOW, YOU LET HIM IN. WHAT TIME IS IT, ANYWAY?"

"I DID?"

"OR MAYBE I DID."

They didn't seem to mind my presence, so I took a seat and watched the game show where contestants tried to make each other cry. A young, gleaming man was on, describing the enchantments his sister used to weave on her pawnshop violin. She'd practice for hours, and the sound of it helped him to concentrate on his schoolwork. "I used to drive her to her lessons way across town, and while she was in there I'd play ball with some guys in this other neighborhood," he said, as the onscreen clock indicated one minute left to go. "One of the guys started looking at Maria for, like, too long. I told him to quit once and he said he wanted to do more than just look, and I'm like oh my God that's my sister." Plumply wholesome, the young man's opponent sat in a blue chair, her feet forming a V.

"So my sister started smiling back at this guy, and I don't know if she even like liked him or whatever, but I wasn't okay with that. She's my sister. My only sister." The clock said thirty seconds, but he wasn't rushing. A three-time champ, he paced his attack in increments.

Mr. Deer said, "WHOSE SISTER?"

Mrs. Deer answered, "HE ONLY HAS ONE SISTER, I THINK."

" . . . then one time she comes out of her lesson carrying her case, and this guy is coming over to her and saying things I couldn't hear . . . [*looking down*] And I'm like, 'Get in the car, Maria,' and she's like, 'Come on,' and then he's like, 'Come on.' But I tell her to get in the car again, and this time I kind of help her in . . . [*looking down, shaking his head*]. But she wasn't all the way in, but I didn't know that. Right? Not until I slammed the car door . . . [*looking down, shaking his head, closing his eyes*]. I rose slowly and slipped unnoticed towards the Deers' bedroom. And there on the ground, in the dirt . . . [*looking down, shaking his head, closing his eyes, and covering them with his hands*] was her finger."

"This is ridiculous," I observed. "The champion has an unfair edge. The more tragedies you hear about, the easier they are to take. It's like when you go away to college and build a tolerance for alcohol," but my companions either didn't hear or didn't care.

The opponent leaned forward slightly, smiling sickly. The camera was tight on her brown eyes, dry as lightbulbs.

Slipping out of the family room, I found what I was looking for on the nightstand, in the middle of a pile of catalogues. The bed was unmade, and there were three different mounds of laundry from what seemed to be three different loads, each half-folded.

January 20, 2020

THANK YOU FOR YOUR CO-OPERATION!

As one of the select families in our pilot utility rededication program, you are helping Drixa and the City of Chicago to evaluate the success of its electric, emergency, television, water, HVAC (heating, venting, and air-conditioning), and telephone systems. During the program, your service in one or more of these systems may be substituted with an indistinguishable simulation. As a thanks for your participation, all of your utility bills will be paid by Drixa. Send in the consent postcard today to get started!

Needless to say, the postcard was missing.

The TV host appeared, tears streaking diagonally from each eye. "I'm sorry. I'm so, so sorry," she said. "But you don't receive any points for that wonderful, awful story. It looks like we're going to have to move on to a speed round." She looked into the camera. "Okay, we're going to take a break and I'm going to splash water on my face [*appreciative chuckles from the studio audience*]." I took my place back on the couch, the Deer letter tucked snugly in my front pants pocket. "And when we come back we'll start round 3 of The Crying Game." The music bloated and died, and the first commercial showed a young boy seated at a picnic table alone on a sun-dappled lawn. Butterflies danced around him as he spread peanut butter and jam on a slice of white bread. A bunch of green grapes caught the sun and gave off a medicinal glow. After a few bites of the sandwich, the boy reached for a plastic cup of foil-sealed liquid. Out of anticipation rather than fear, he took his time peeling back the foil and then drank down the contents with a contentment that bordered on obscene. "It's not water," he promised the camera "It's H_2O."

"WHAT IS THAT, A BOY OR A PUPPET?" the man muttered.

"LOOK AT HIS SKIN!"

"FAKE WATER, FAKE KID."

Meanwhile the voiceover explained how Drixa had perfected the technology for synthesizing H_2O, "the new water," available soon in select neighborhoods by subscription only. For less than the price of cable, you could wash, clean, and cook with complete peace of mind.

There was no reason to stay here. I made for the door, and they followed me out. "What makes you think there's something wrong with H_2O?" I asked from the front steps. "H_2O is chemically purer than water. It's good stuff, it's going to save lives."

"Or maybe it'll make my boobs grow." Mr. Deer's upper lip was protecting his teeth.

"Exactly," Mrs. Deer agreed. "Or your balls drop off."

"Your what? Where do you get that?"

Mrs. Deer grunted. "Between the Drixa commercials every five minutes and the flyers every day in the mail, who knows what to believe?" Her husband slid his upper lip up and down over his teeth.

"If you'll just give me a few minutes of your time, I think I can clear this all up. I'm a scientist with Drixa Labs. Chief Engineer, actually, and those flyers you're receiving . . . I'd be very much interested in possibly seeing—"

"I thought you said you were lost," Mrs. Deer said.

"I thought you had to take a piss."

"He did, I heard him."

"That might have been me, actually." Mr. Deer angled his body towards the doorway. "I'm sorry, I don't remember your name, but you've caught us at a bad time. Now if you don't mind . . . " His face hardened.

"Here," said his wife, thrusting a piece of goldenrod paper at me.

"The name's Hayden Shivers," I reminded him, shaking my head at the plastic deer as I departed—with real purpose to my step, as the urge to urinate had resurged.

CHAPTER TWELVE

It was less than six weeks earlier that Yemina had first appeared at my door with a bundle the size of a decent pumpkin and stuffed with clothes, a pocket dictionary, and a photo album—presumably her family though she never showed me. I suppose the fact that I never asked denotes some crucial lack of affection, but the way she threw herself so completely into my life, doting on Hayden Jr. and fiercely admiring her new employer and taking such an avid interest in his research, suggests that she preferred not to dwell on the life she left behind. It would perhaps be more forgiving than I deserve to call me generous for taking her in, but the effect was unquestionably healthy.

The thing about Ginelle was that she depended on me so little. So I'd pretend not to need her either, just to break even. We had once done little favors for each other, but this stopped after Hayden Jr. came, when we tacitly agreed that the only reason for doing favors (my picking her up at the train station, her ironing my shirts) was the pat on the back. But with the phony warmth dispensed with, nothing filled the vacuum, not warmth, not coldness, just a tepid coexistence. The reductio ad absurdum was sex: why knock yourself out trying to get me off when I can do it better myself? I mean sure, that's good, thanks. And if you ever need a hand. No? You're okay? Me too, I'm okay. But thanks for asking.

The first days with Yemina were slightly awkward because she didn't seem to understand her purpose or even how she'd got there, but eventually the arrangement was communicated without being spelled out. The biggest surprise was how natural the domestic arrangement came to feel—more natural, I would argue, than what I'd had with Ginelle.

Hayden Jr. accepted the stranger's presence without hesitation. I remember in particular one midnight encounter. He descended the stairs, his hollow eyes and pale complexion reminiscent of all those Spielberg kids you've seen. "Are you thirsty, Hay?" I motioned for the boy to sit at the kitchen table and took a Country Life from the refrigerator. There was tenderness, almost pity, in his obedience, but not admiration.

"Can I go down to the basement?" he asked.

"Not tonight, Hay, no. It's a mess down there. As soon as I clean up, okay?"

Hayden Jr. rolled his can of lemonade back and forth on the table, trying to determine how far the can went on one complete rotation. He kept one finger where the sun was on the label, just in case the image repeated itself.

"What are you building, anyway?"

"It's a project for work. Just a filter. You know what I do, right? Drains and filters?" Suddenly inspired to demonstrate rather than explain something I didn't quite understand, I popped the can open, turned it upside-down and swept my arm over the table letting the lemonade spill out into an oblong puddle. Now the boy was captivated. "We're going to pretend this is the Chicago River. Ych, right? And this," I said, reaching for a striped tea towel, "is Drixa."

"Drixa's going to wipe up the lemonade."

"Now remember, we're pretending the lemonade is the Chicago River—dirty, smelly, and poisonous. What if there was something that turned the lemonade into water? Drixa's not just going to wipe up the Chicago River," I said, soaking up the spill with the towel. "It's going to make it safe to drink." I wrung the towel into the glass, explaining, "Now you really have to use your imagination, because we have to pretend the glass is full of pure, clean water."

"I like lemonade."

"Yes, but look, not only is there water in the glass, but thanks to a smart man on his way to becoming Chief Engineer, there's more water there than there used to be lemonade."

"I like lemonade, Dad."

Yemina held her hand out for the towel. "Well, good, you like lemonade. We have lots for you. But pretend for a second that we're almost out of cans. How would that make you feel?"

"Bad," Hayden said.

"What if every time I squeezed the towel, enough cold lemonade came out to fill your glass and mine too?"

"Every time?"

"Every time!"

"We'd never run out!"

Yemina made things simple. And I didn't jump every time she entered the room.

There was no language problem, but occasionally she had trouble catching on to the way I put things. For example, she didn't realize at first that when I said, "What's new," I didn't really expect a response other than "not much."

Or: "Why do you make that sound, 'woo-hoo'?"

"Don't you have *The Simpsons* in Zimbabwe?

"No. Zambia, Hayden."

"Anyway, it's a cartoon show on TV, for adults. Do you know what a cartoon is?"

"Yes, but I didn't know they were for adults."

"I think it's for adults," I said. "And when Homer gets excited, he says 'woo-hoo.' Usually when I say it I'm being facetious."

"What is facetious?"

"When you say something and don't mean it. You say it in a certain way to show you don't mean it, but I suppose the other person has to pick up on the signal. Do you have that where you come from?"

"Yes, of course."

Yemina never made a mistake twice. She was quick, kind, and a good maid. She bought me a fabulous pink button-down shirt, no collar, with tortoise-shell buttons, similar to the one that Lionel Dawson wore in his publicity photo. Also, she had inordinate mechanical capability, repairing the browning function on the microwave oven, subduing the washer rumble during the spin cycle, and rebuilding a cantankerous sump pump.

"Are you a virgin?" I asked one night.

"No." She shimmied her shoulders. "Do you want me to be?"

"You don't have to answer. It's a rhetorical question." I couldn't get enough of her skin. The shadowy hollows behind each clavicle, the shift from brown to pink on the sides of the hands and feet. I pretended not to notice the emotional component of our lovemaking, until late one Sunday night, three weeks after her arrival.

The condom made a difference. I knew it was ridiculous to rely on a thin layer of latex—which, after all, was designed to let the sensation through—for insulation against cheating. (As for birth control, Snowflake took care to outfit all its girls with implants.) But sex without a condom was undeniably a degree more intimate, a pleasure I had never enjoyed with anyone besides Ginelle. This slight measure of fidelity seemed to sadden and vex Yemina, but she never mentioned it. It was enough to appease my weak guilt reflex. No more than a thin membrane separated anything from anything else. Pinching the condom's slimy lip, I pulled myself out. This physical uncorking had a verbal consequence that took me by surprise.

"I love you," she said. "And I don't mean that facetiously."

I hesitated. Just now I'd intended to skip into the bathroom, dispose of the condom, and take a leak, but the situation demanded a reply.

"I love," I started. A stolen glance at the clock radio: 11:58. One of those times I always seemed to catch. 12:34, 10:17, 11:58. It would probably be 11:58 when I'd look at a clock for the last time—but not this time.

"Everything about you," I finished.

Yemina looked down. "You better do something with that thing. And do you think there's any Fudge Sludge left in the freezer?"

She fixed her hair while I scooped. "When are you going to show me the basement? Do you keep another girlfriend down there?"

"It's kind of a mess, really."

"So you admit it, you're making a girl out of wires and ice cream."

"Something like that."

"Hayden, tell me about your science project. Really. What's all that noise? Can't you make her quieter?"

"Sorry."

"It's okay," she said. "But really."

"Now? How do I even put this? When something passes through something, it's not the same anymore, and when water passes through a filter, it's not the same water anymore. Once it goes through the filter, you can try to reintroduce what you've filtered out, but probably it won't dissolve."

I took Yemina's hand in mine. Her skin was the color of cinnamon-sugar, mine very white. The way they were clasped reminded me of a graphic icon for racial harmony. But that was for white Americans and black Americans. Yemina was an African. And I wasn't just harmonizing with her, I was colonizing her. Asserting my superiority and wiping out centuries of heritage, all in the name of adulterous whim. This idea shriveled my penis, and it shivered in a cold puddle of arousal gone bad. I was afraid to face her face, but then I felt breath on my ear. The hollows bordered by her collarbones and her shoulders could each hold three tablespoons of water. Without words, she was telling me that she knew what this meant, in all its political and historical dimensions. She understood that when our lips met, she'd become infected with the virus of Western Civ. Maybe the surrender was never offered ignorantly, not ever.

I squeezed Yemina's hand and let go. "You look very comfortable."

"Yes, I could stay in bed all day."

"Why don't you? Take the day off, Yemina. You deserve it."

"Woo-hoo," she said.

"In fact, maybe I'll do the same thing. Would you like that?"

"Take Hayden Jr. to school, then go to work. You still have a job, don't you? Today I'm staying in bed. Maybe tomorrow you can stay in bed while I work."

"This is an individual sport, then."

"Pardon?"

"You don't want company."

"No, I don't want company. It's okay. It's just that today I woke up and felt the whole world is lonely. Why get out of bed on a day like this?"

"You're depressed."

"What is depressed?"

"It's a spirit that takes hold of you, makes you tired and hopeless, afraid of the future, sick of yourself."

"No. I am not depressed. I hope I never feel depressed."

Never let it be said that I denied Yemina's contribution to the invention of H_2O. If I had understood precisely what it was, I would have mentioned it soon enough. Reputation matters to me, of course, but that's just it: my reputation stands to gain by people discovering how I nurtured the native genius (a term I use advisedly) of this woeful refugee girl.

And don't call Yemina my muse. Don't flatter me like that, don't insult her. Every invention from fire on down has had multiple inventors—rivals, companions, keepers of mutual secrets, sharers in ignorant fate. But history demands the genius. Drixa needed me to wear the mantle, and undoubtedly the nod satisfied something sour in me, a hunger for recognition or at least an expectation of being included in the list of thank-yous.

Her brother used to work for a plumber, she explained, which caught me off guard since there was no plumbing in the place I pictured her girlhood. But then of course it would be even harder to imagine such a bright, colorful mind springing up in a culture without hot and cold water on demand. Archimides was merely the first scientist to draw inspiration from the bath. With a little fiddling, Yemina doubled the pressure in the shower, and an ingenious network of rubber tubing she installed kept the humidifier full.

Some excerpts from my admittedly scattershot laboratory notes reliably narrate the progress in the basement:

Date	Variable(s)	Gain (oz.)	Comments
12/15	.2 gm NaCl; 30°C	.01	Fifty times that amount last week. What's different now?
12/22	Prefiltering source water through standard charcoal purifier	.12	Within 20 minutes of arriving in basement, Y not only grasped the concept but improved efficiency 1200%
1/1/20	UV exposure	.09	"Remember the man who drank water between the afternoon prayer and the evening prayer. The angel of death came and slew him, because he drank when the dead were drinking and so was a robber of the dead. Therefore it is forbidden." (Talmud)

1/04	Barometer 24 in.	.05	Trial and error has its limitations. Sometimes the most scientifically astute step to be taken is called quitting. That's where partners come in. Holmes had his Watson. Alexander Graham Bell had his . . . Watson. Crick, too. Someone to say: Needle? With all due respect, sir, that's not even a haystack.
1/17	Prefiltering; 35°C	.11	Waters of the dead? That sounds like water from a past time. How is the future populated by the dead? If we kill it, that's how.
1/19	Prefiltering; 35°C; agitation.	.07	Some puzzles have no answers. You actually want to bite your own head.
1/26	Nuking the fungus	NA	Dripping sound behind caught my attention, and I looked up to find water sliding down the walls, the ceiling soaked through. Ecstatic, I raced upstairs to tell Y and H Jr., only to find them on the floor, deeply immersed in a game of Sorry! oblivious to the overflowing tub. Y: What is it? H: Nothing. The tub. Y: What are you doing down there? H: The fungus was in the microwave HJr.: What are you trying to do? Kill it?

2/1	Prefiltering; vibration (Y's suggestion, again)	.25	The key of course is the modulator, which adjusts the vibration from the handle via three sliding switches stolen from the graphic equalizer of a stereo system. It took more than a few hours to assemble a wand, but none approaches the effectiveness of that first prototype, which I'm still hoping will turn up somewhere.

I can still remember how the filter of the wand was coated with fresh fungus, how we wordlessly bore it to the sink for a demonstration of its power. Our eyes locked briefly in a passionate yet professional embrace. There were two drinking glasses of equal size. I filled one up and prepared to pour its contents through the filter and into the other. Yemina depressed the button on the handle and then adjusted the modulator to account for I'm not sure which factors. The expertise belonged to her. When the hum had attained the proper level, her eyes narrowed, and I tilted the glass and watched the water hit the filter.

All of those afternoons at the movies, absorbing plots thirstily, trying to stimulate the part of my brain that worked on problems when I wasn't paying them attention. It worked every so often, too, and the sketches and formulae that emerged this way usually emerged in a completed state. New ideas gave me a feeling of relief, something like cracking my neck. Yet all those movies, maybe they had infected me with their unrealism, amnesia, and expectation of climax, finally leaving me irrational as a holy man.

We made progress together, or at least that's what I thought. Our bodies surged and splashed into one another.

Yemina sat at the dining room table with me as I worked. I had books open, one laptop computer hooked up to the Web and another set up for taking notes and filling in data. Occasionally, I swore under my breath when I misplaced a file or when a Web site took too long to come up. At this, she looked up from the two-month-old copy of a kitchenware catalogue that she'd been reading for two months, and I made a tender face at her to assure that it wasn't she that invoked my wrath. She went back to reading about a dehydrator, for making jerky, raisins, whatever.

"Superior airflow," the text promised. "Uniform, consistent drying of fish, fruit, and fowl."

She seemed content there, and I dropped any sense of obligation to entertain her. Of course, I never suspected she was scanning the data on the screens, let alone that she was making any sense of them.

Yemina never ate my cooking. I'd stuffed cornish hens, basted chicken wings with margarine and Tabasco, grilled turkey burgers with onions and green peppers. Finally, she'd told me she didn't eat birds. She only smiled when I asked her if it was some kind of religious belief. It was okay with me—I didn't eat eggs. From then on, we had fishsticks almost every night. It became a joke with us.

"Fishsticks, dear?"

"Yes, fishsticks."

"Are you sure you wouldn't like a bucket of fried chicken?"

"No. Fishsticks."

As I pondered data, Yemina slipped on her Keds and wandered around the house. Or, not exactly wandered, because she knew her destination, she just didn't head there immediately.

After reorganizing the stack of magazines into his (Quantum Mechanics, Particle Physics, Nearmissology) and hers (Williams-Sonoma, Viking Ovens), she crept down the stairs and pulled the string that lit up my laboratory. It smelled good down there, like a thunderstorm. The instruments were cool to the touch. Yemina plugged in a cord that connected to a chrome-plated box with a rubber lid. A low hum filled the room.

CHAPTER THIRTEEN

Miyumi Park caught up with me in front of the Brahms and led me to a dim corner of the atrium, where a pair of easy chairs faced each other beneath the mother-of-pearl face of a grandfather clock stuck at almost noon or almost midnight. Or maybe not stuck. Without a pendulum swinging or a second hand sweeping, I couldn't tell.

"Lionel needs that letter from you."

"Can I just wash up first?"

"He needs it for a marketing meeting in Vegas. Lionel doesn't like to leave things to the last minute. The event planners are reviewing every detail of the launch. Did you get the schedule?"

"Nobody said there was a schedule."

"The media prefer it that way." She produced a trifold sheet and let me hold it long enough to see but not enough to read.

Crowd assembles:	2:00-2:30
PAL arrives with HS:	2:30
PAL offers to drive HS away:	2:33
AB comes into view:	2:34
MoC begins address ("A Somber Anniversary"):	2:35
WS asks "Anniversary of what?":	2:37
LD begins address ("Acts of Unmistakable Genius"):	2:40
LD invites HS to podium:	2:43
LD invites OW to podium:	2:43:30
PAL pushes HS forward:	2:44
Ambulance arrives:	2:45
HS down:	2:46

"Everyone said the rehearsal went very well," I said.

"You did just great, Hayden. Is that what you want me to say? You fell real good. Here's a copy of the letter." She slid it into the front pocket of my pants.

I grasped her wrist before she could withdraw her hand. "Come upstairs with me."

She blinked. "I'm sure if you have any questions I can answer them just as well down here."

"This is a hotel," I maintained. "That's what you do in hotels. You invite up to your room."

"What about the bio?"

"We know who I am."

"Let's not get ahead of ourselves," she said.

"Can I ask something though?"

She blinked again.

"Who do you work for?"

"I work for you."

"Already?"

"Soon enough."

"The company or the protestors?"

"Both."

"Do they both know that?"

"Of course. Nobody wants their toes stepped on these days. As Human Resource Director, I act as liaison, finding and strengthening common interests and values. Liberty, for instance. Free thought, free expression, and that includes freedom to criticize your employer. What are you doing when you erect an artificial wall against participating in ICE-9 activities? You're begging your people to spy and blow their whistles. Walls are membranes, and membranes are permeable."

"Some of the protestors are on the Drixa payroll?" I asked.

"If that's how they choose to engage with the company, we're okay with that."

"They're out there distributing literature," I said, proffering a limp leaflet.

$H_2NO!$
an oral history of the shame

see-through
the transparent plot
to take away something free
and replace it with
an ugly chemical
should make you sick
if you have a heart
—paula d., willowbrook

wake up!
remember water?
remember how it felt on skin?
remember how it used to smell?
think back, if you can,
to the days before
the waters of forgetfulness
—james j., oakpoint

dying wish
when thirst quenches me
and my body grows cold
plant no daisies on my grave
raise no glass in my name
shed no tears for me
if it means using H_2O
—aqua b., water street

"Hayden, that's what protestors do," she said as she scanned appreciatively. "We underwrite the printing. "

"So the launch is this Friday?"

"Yes."

"Whether I sign or not. No more tests?"

"The only way to test the product is to launch it. Any sample less than the total population would distort the outcome."

"So you're free to launch just anything."

"Free? We're obligated. Anything else would mean withholding valuable, life-saving information. No, everything must be disclosed without hesitation. Absolute transparency is a given for Lionel. This letter of agreement will be entered in the public record. Send it to the *Tribune* if you wish."

"I need to go upstairs," I said, no longer betraying any hope that she might join me. I just wanted to get away from her (and, of course, to urinate). If she called after me, it wasn't very loud.

First I started hot water in the sink. Then I relieved my bladder. Then I picked up the phone and ordered a bowl of ice cream from room service. Vanilla, chocolate, and strawberry—the Holy Trinity. And then I returned to the bathroom and shaved. The pores of my face stung, and this somehow stimulated a thinking process that went beyond the linear, and I felt destined for better things now. Sure, it was egomaniacal, but I always knew I would become a symbol, not that I'd accomplish anything myself, but symbolism would be cast over me like a net. The Great Casting Agent in the Sky would give me the role of symbol. Symbol of *what* was the question. I splashed some Brahms aftershave on my face and stared into the mirror thinking about how my face would look in the papers.

Personally, I hadn't done so bad. *Considering*. When I looked at myself realistically and called a truce in the eternal struggle between *why me?* (I don't deserve this) and *why not me?* (I deserve more than this), I hadn't done all that bad.

When I emerged from the steamy bathroom, the TV was on, with the Brahms playing, with information about the services available to guests. Massage. Hypnotherapy, aromatherapy, group therapy, Debtors Anonymous. *The Brahms Reading Circle is discussing Luther Brahms's The Best Rest tomorrow at 9 a.m. Coffee enemas every Thursday morning in the Holistic Health Center.* The scrolling messages entranced me so much that I didn't respond to a knock on the door.

Possessed by a strange feeling that Luther Brahms (1871–1917) would have something momentous to say, I leapt toward the dresser.

The Best Rest:
An Ode to Hotels
By Luther Brahms

Sometimes a book will do the trick. There was a time when I read voraciously—books that had been adapted for film and books about the art of film. Film encyclopedias. Then I found seduction, and books seemed like stale kisses for the lonely. Then I fell in love and became a husband and father, and fatherhood makes you a permanent fool: all that peek-a-boo.

This book was deep green and had a pebbled cover embossed with gold. The first line on the first page was "The instant you enter a hotel, you become a greater man." A previous guest had used a ballpoint pen to circle these words. "Beautiful women become more beautiful in hotels" (p. 3). "If somebody dies in one of my rooms, I pay all funeral expenses" (p. 31). "More than one guest has told me he's doubled his wealth in the course of a single stay at the Brahms. I say there's something in the pillows" (p. 122). This was written before Salim Sultan's magnificent film adaptation of Horacio Quiroga's short story, "The Feather Pillow," where a bloodsucking monster lurks inside.

There was a second knock at the door, and I took the bowl from the person standing there, proving that you don't always look at the person serving you in a hotel.

"Enjoy your ice cream, sir."

And then I turned around.

CHAPTER FOURTEEN

She didn't want to speak in the room and wordlessly directed me to put on a white bathrobe and a pair of dark sunglasses. I took one quick bite of each flavor, changed clothes, and climbed into the wheelchair that she had brought with her.

Another woman in a wheelchair rode the elevator with us. It was a tight fit, and I found myself smiling stupidly, wondering whether we were supposed to acknowledge each other. Down in the lobby there were more wheelchairs. A man with a white cane tapped by. Another man with a dog, a smallish terrier you wouldn't usually associate with the blind.

I counted six blind people in the lobby and another eight or nine in wheelchairs. They were upbeat, chatting with each other and with their companions, checking their watches and looking up toward the skylight, watching the clouds grow pink.

We settled in a far corner, out of earshot, but neither of us said a word as the room filled. She took me by the hand, but I didn't know whether it was a true gesture or part of the act. "Are you surprised to see me?" she said, bouncing a little in her Keds.

"Is that a trick question?" I said, but then she squeezed my fingers like she needed me to be serious.

More or less everybody wore slippers and loose-fitting gowns, all white or nearly white pastels. We were at capacity, but it didn't feel the least bit congested. One minute the architecture felt companionable, homey, the next it raised ecclesiastical hairs on your spine. The rest of the city, the past and the future, all disappeared down a hole.

"I'm just glad you're not mad at me," she said.

"Mad, no. Yemina, you don't have to explain to me why you left. If you have something to say, I'm listening, but it's your decision."

"Do you mean that?"

"You were always free to go and come as you pleased."

"Right. I went."

Hotel employees circulated, carrying coolers filled with lemonade cans. Others helped guests into chairs and fetched footstools and headrests. Soft music, somewhere between Tuvan gurgle and Sufi chant, wafted around us, melting away muscular tension.

"Don't worry, I wasn't with those people. And if I was, it would have been okay. You don't have to worry about me."

"I can't help it. You're my lab partner . . . No, you're more." I left it ambiguous whether I meant she was more to me, emotionally, or more than a partner, that is., that her contribution was greater than half.

"Your science project was important to me, but you and Hayden Jr. were more important. Maybe I shouldn't say that." She squeezed my hand to signal that I listen, for once.

"I am younger than you." Yemina said, "but I feel old. My path from Africa to Chicago made me an old woman. It was good luck to find you, but beside that nothing else was lucky. It doesn't matter now, I am trying to forget."

The surrounding towers dimmed their lights, and street lamps were extinguished so that the Brahms could glow on its own. The atmosphere had been regulated to a premodern, pagan level, and I wondered if supplemental oxygen was coming out of the vents, but all I caught when I sniffed the air was the lightest lavender essence.

"If I didn't come here, you and Ginelle wouldn't be divorcing, so maybe you caught my bad luck. I would take it back if I could. That's why I went to see your friend Julian."

"He's not my friend, he's my lawyer."

"I found his card in the house and arranged to meet him. He insisted that I bring the prototype and requested a demonstration. When I arrived at his office he poured me a glass of vintage water."

—Tell me, Yemina, how long have you been in Chicago?

—Six months only.

—Your English is so good already.

—English is spoken in Zambia.

—Of course it is. Now, tell me about the science project. I understand that encouraging prospects have turned out to be singular phenomena. Flukes.

—What about their marriage?

—When the cat is dead, you don't keep feeding it. What about his science project?

The river flowing under the hotel seemed to hold still for a moment.

"I told him the truth," Yemina continued. "It works very well now."

"There was more to it than we thought at first," I agreed. "The vibration, that was everything."

"Not quite. Something else, too, activates the fungus."

"Namely . . . "

"I call it a dry snap. When humidity suddenly dropped by more than 10 percent, the normal metabolic functions go dormant."

"Like hibernation?" I asked.

"The fungus has been doing this for millions of years. The dehydrator just accentuates the process."

"Just as pain can produce pleasure, drought can produce moisture."

"I don't think he's a good lawyer."

"No, he is a good lawyer," I said. "But a bad influence. Who did Julian introduce you to?"

"A man from Drixa, his name was Lionel. They brought me to their labs, but I said I preferred to work in your basement, where I could be there for Hayden Jr. when he got home from school."

"And he promised to make you very rich. That's what you deserve. Tens of millions of homes, hundreds of millions of gallons."

"Stop, Hayden, I'm depressed already. The waters could be very harmful."

"Nonsense, the test subjects are doing wonderfully. H_2O is water."

"Listen, they could be harmful. I have done some calculations."

The next hour was difficult for me. She refused to write anything down, and the concepts were knotty, and even familiar concepts like isotopes and the difference between exponential and geometric growth were deployed in unexpected ways. I felt like was back in school, but this time instead of earning a steady B+/A–, I was flat-out flunking. And it served me right; while I'd been angling for my big promotion, Yemina had leaped eons ahead. Gradually, the scene she was sketching came into focus:

"Tell me again how the fungus makes water," I said.

"That's what I've been trying to tell you. It doesn't do what we thought it does; it makes hydrogen, which bonds with oxygen, to form water."

"Where does the hydrogen come from?"

"When activated, the fungus breaks atmospheric oxygen and nitrogen up to make hydrogens, which then bond with other oxygens."

"You created an accelerator down in the basement," I said, thinking I had grasped her point.

"The fungus does it all," she said. "That's what it was made to do, you just have to treat it right."

"What can we do now, Yemina?"

"If these molecules could be tagged."

"Of course," I said. "That's what I would do."

"We need to screen them out so they don't pass through the filter a second time."

"A kind of shield."

"You understand what I'm talking about."

"I'm glad you're safe," I said. "Don't tell me where, but do you have access to an adequate laboratory?"

"It won't be simple," she said. "We've already separated the fungus from its soil, and now you want to pry out its secrets. That's not kind."

"I appreciate your concern," I said, though, frankly, I thought it was nuts to care about the fungus this way. Looking back, however, it's clear that such concern accounted for Yemina's H_2O harvest being so much greater and so much more consistent than mine. The same goes for talking to houseplants.

"It won't be simple," she repeated.

"But you'll do it, for the sake of science."

"I don't understand what that means, but I'll try, for the sake of the fungus and the sake of the water."

"The device you describe would mean a great deal to Drixa, and whoever should invent it would be in for a rich reward." Here I sounded to myself just like Lionel Dawson; the supervisory responsibilities of Chief Engineer had been thrust upon me.

She squeezed my hand again, this time to tell me to shut up and watch as the moonlight streamed through the atrium, turning every person and stick of furniture a gleaming, glassy white. The room became warmer, hushed, and ever-so-slightly larger. Neither particle nor wave, the light assumed a pure liquid quality. Nobody was astonished when I rose from my wheelchair, pocketed the shades, and tried the exit . . . but the door was bolted. I actually panicked for a moment before noticing the Please Use Revolving Door sign.

There was no doubt that the blind Argentine architect of the Brahms was a genius. The experience in the atrium had gone far beyond the aesthetic. It threw the past few weeks into stark relief, and, surveying it all as if from a slight elevation, I saw to my surprise that nothing was missing. My memory was free (or as free as ever) from gaps: it was just that I had been too caught up in things to comprehend it all at once. The realization left me with simultaneous relief and panic.

Chapter Fifteen

Soon I was aboard the train to Las Vegas. Julian was there, and more importantly, so was Lionel. The man across the aisle read a pamphlet with a ridiculous ferocity, holding it so close to his face that he must have expected the words to jump into his eyes. He left it on his seat when the train reached Michigan City.

Listen to the Snow

Have you realized yet that water is a living thing with feelings and a memory? All water remembers, but ice and snow have the longest memories, especially snow. The information those crystals store can be retrieved centuries later. If we know now how the dinosaurs died or when fish began to walk on land, it's because the snow told us. *Drixa Snow-Cones. One of the Many Ways That Drixa Puts the Awe in Water. Now available in raspberry and pineapple.*

Balling the leaflet in my fist, I flashed on a B-movie I'd seen in college, a monster flick starring snow—not a snowman but a malevolent ion that animated snow crystals into a wintertime strangler. Authorities puzzle over the snapped necks of pretty young ski bunnies, ignoring the nearby puddles and water stains. At first, the scenes of violence reveal little, but with every death a little more of the killer is shown. In a flashback, it emerges that the ski lodge was built on the site of a high-security prison; a horrible blizzard comes, and all the inmates suffocate under a blanket of white while the warden and guards escape by helicopter.

The town's renegade cop uncovers the ugly truth and sets out across the bleak winter landscape to evacuate the lodge, but a rapid snowdrift capsizes his vehicle and punches a hole through the windshield. The crack of a pistol is heard and then a choked cry. The final image, of the red siren poking through a crust of snow like a nipple or Japanese flag, is held for a full minute before the credits roll.

The audience laughed at Silent Snow, Deadly Snow's sledge-hammer script and blowdryer acting, but I confess I was left shaken. From then on, I always feared the snow a little, something I kept to myself when I moved from the West Coast to Princeton and then to Chicago.

The train took the track in sips, like water up a straw.
Before long, I arrived in another city that was not really another city. What Las Vegas had become at the end of the twentieth century was what Chicago was shaping up to be at the start of the twenty-first: capital of simulation and simulation of capital, a kind of four-dimensional abacus of bodies and values.

With New York and Los Angeles replicated, shrunken, and transplanted to midwestern soil, it came as no surprise when Las Vegas itself reappeared on the eastern shore of Lake Michigan, complete with hailstones among other plagues. In the wake of catastrophe, the architecture of recreation became the new language of homesickness, belated civic pride. The winter-strafed Sin City enjoyed the greatest success of all the rebuilt cities. Bets took on a coating of respectability in the age of Nearmissology, with its complex probabilities. It was the logical place to find Julian. He was not so much a gambler as slave to the new science. Depending on the university, it was the department of either Nearmissology or Closecallology, each discipline insisting that it approached catastrophe from a distinct philosophy.

Closecallologists liked to say that while their rivals analyzed near-miss events as predictors of disaster, they sought to understand them as causes. Nearmissologists disputed these terms. It was hard to tell them apart; both called on specialists from various other disciplines—Urban Planning, Statistics, Theoretical Physics, Ecology—to analyze slimly avoided disasters. Warnings issued in the journals carried a lot of weight with the media and some governments that had become inured to the usual reports of plane crashes and environmental illness. Everyone knew that forty to sixty passenger planes crashed every year, but when the American Journal of Closecallology revealed that ten times that number almost crashed, nearly causing well over five thousand deaths annually, the calls to overhaul the industry reached a crescendo.

Nearmissology, the study of events that almost happened but didn't, became fashionable just as news of the its approach hit the papers. The new discipline blurred reality and possibility, fueling nationwide panic and giving rise to the reactivation of aborted plans for a missile defense system. Billions of dollars poured into an emergency test of the system despite protests over the expense and the overwhelming likelihood of failure. These objections were met with a further bastardization of Nearmissology claiming that, at certain speeds, failure and success were interchangeable terms.

Through all the debates Nearmissologists agreed on one point. Near misses dramatically increased the chances of something actually happening. You could find a near miss lurking in the recent past of every great catastrophe, if you knew where to look.

I lived in the future. I could travel to Las Vegas or Hollywood or Orlando without leaving Chicago, but I could never leave Chicago any more than I could leave the universe.

My first visit felt unnervingly rather than reassuringly familiar. As I stepped off the El, the city's phantasmagoria of shimmering lights failed to dazzle even a little. The drawbridge leading into the Snows Hotel struck me as much less ingenious that it should have been. The requisite red carpet could stand a shampoo. The marble staircase wound around a fake waterfall—no water at all but an elaborately orchestrated light-and-sound production. The sham had an immediate and authentic effect on my bladder. By the time I spotted my quarry at the craps table, my mood was just the opposite of what the hotel had hoped to engineer.

"How's the action?" I asked.

"At the moment, odds are 7:1 against a natural disaster somewhere on the planet before midnight, central time. That's where my money is tonight."

"Anywhere in the world? Conditions have been approaching disaster lately?"

"No, it just feels like earthquake weather to me."

"Let me ask you this." I said. "What are the odds that Drixa is filtering bad water?"

"So? I thought that's what filters were for."

"These filters don't filter. You know they're not made for that."

"What kind of damage are we talking?"

"Probably insignificant, but possibly incalculable. Every new solution raises the specter of a new and more terrible disaster. The only thing that can get us out of the water crisis is a new and more terrible one."

"And you're here why?"

"I just wish things were different."

"Yeah. Well, they aren't."

"I need to talk to Mayor King."

"And what do you expect from him? Mayor King's just like you and me."

"You mean he operates on little more than vanity and fear?"

"Yes, fear, his own fear. Don't you remember the time he got up on top of his limo during the riots? And no sound issued from his throat? His voice was paralyzed with fear, and the crowd somehow saw themselves for what they had become, a mob, and shamefully, peacefully dispersed."

"He got lucky that time," I agreed.

"That comet missed us by a million miles and made me a rich man."

The notion of harvesting water from comets dated back to one of the more far-fetched justifications for a satellite-based missile defense system. The military argued that wayward comets and asteroids could potentially do more damage than enemy volleys, and what's more, these things could now be predicted. It might take a while before the next comet menaced earth, they argued, but by that time it would be too late to start preparing.

The political debate over the expense and risk of building the cometary defense system had entered one of its many deadlocks when Lionel Dawson called a press conference announcing hard evidence of an imminent strike in the Chicagoland area and revealing Drixa's advanced state of readiness to defend city and planet. "We're in the water business, after all," noted Dawson. "And what is a comet if not a big dirty snowball?" He promised not only protection from the threat but a free glass of cometary water for all of the city's 40 million citizens. The technology under development would save the world and solve the hydrocrisis in one fell swoop, though Drixa's perennial bugbear had a few choice words.

Where Is Drixa's Dirty Snowball?
Warne Shoals

"Soon." "Next year." "Before too long." "Before it's too late." When they promise, we believe. We trust data and satellite pictures. Granted, the water-bearing comet might come. Our water shortage might end just like that. Drixa asks us to have faith, so we do. Drixa instructs us to be patient, and we comply, right? So far, neither our patience nor their excuses have doomed us. Patience and excuses, however, do not a sound water reclamation policy make. Sooner or later, outside experts should be called in to asses the comet.

I, for one, look forward to fixing myself a cup of piping-hot comet-water tea. Just imagine the faint tang of comet dust and Milky Way in your morning cup! Even entertaining such a notion persuades me that we live at a fortunate moment in history. Drixa deserves our gratitude for proposing this bold plan and for orchestrating the necessary science and technology. They even, admittedly, deserve a little more patience while they smooth out the dissonance in all that orchestration. It's just that if nobody questions the wisdom of cometary waiting, Drixa might just make an asteroid of us.

Drixa had promised that new harvesting technologies would resolve the global hydrocrisis, but as the comet approached, scientists realized that even if it did come within striking distance, it would be fat and fast enough to smash any projectile aiming to release its moisture—and possibly to throw the planet off its axis. The company then decided to change the subject rather than delivering the bad news, and hydrosynthesis was born.

"Usually, I bet on the disasters," Julian said. "But everybody saw that one coming, so I knew it would never hit."

"Maybe the next time around," I replied.

"Any word on the black girl?" When I didn't answer, he continued, "I could find her, Hayden. Not me personally, but I know how to find people. Of course, it wouldn't be cheap."

"I'll think about it. But first, what about the mayor?"

With what he seemed to think was a subtle gesture, Julian rotated his whole, ice cream cone shaped body toward the traditional Vegas games. I rose and wended my way past the baccarat tables into a stained-glass-lamplit alcove lined with wood the color of good scotch.

Mayor Theophilus King's offices had relocated to Las Vegas two years earlier. It was meant to be a temporary measure, but favorable circumstances had never materialized, and the administration grew used to the glitz and artifice of this reconstructed minitropolis.

I came upon a gathering of about a dozen people, several of them tall brunettes. One, in a little black number, held a glass of wine in each hand while the mayor performed a card trick for her. She shrieked, "And where *is* the three of clubs?"

"Where *is* the three of clubs," the mayor echoed.

"I don't talk like that!"

Stepping between them, I put a hand on his shoulder. "This is going to be a disaster. Do you want to stop it, or do I have to?"

He looked at me like a dog looks at an encyclopedia. "Pick a card." Close up, his gaunt yet vital features held just as much power as his voice. Those low notes of a dusty Stradivarius.

"Yes, I will, just as soon as I can have your ear for a minute. If we act now, we can prevent a true disaster."

"Are you ever going to pick a card?" the woman said.

I picked a four of diamonds—a losing card if there ever was one. It made me feel so tired that all I wanted to do was to wrap up the prototype like a gift and drop it in the river.

"Preventive measures are outlawed," Mayor King said. "After the farce of the Cometary Defense System, we can react only to *real* disasters, that is, once they have actually happened. And there are enough of those to keep us busy. In fact, we haven't even caught up to 2012 yet."

"But if we act now, there won't be a disaster," I argued.

"Call me in eight years," the mayor said, returning to his party. At the back of the room was a door, which led to another office, one with the Drixa trident logo over the door. Off to one side, two smooth-faced aids stood over a table covered with contact sheets scrawled with slogans and debated the latest Drixa ad campaign.

"How about: 'Drixa: The New Purity.'"

"It's not enough to *say* purity. It's got to *be* pure. A pure transparent message. That's why I like the barefoot girl."

"That photo is so meaningful I can hardly see it through the tears."

"I thought *pure* was still taboo. Can we say *pure* again? In a slogan? These are anxious times. Who wants to be reminded?"

"C'mon, there are reminders everywhere you look. Every form of water, from rain to rivers, reminds you. Get used to it. Capitalize on it. In other words, water advertises water. It's perpetual free marketing."

"Besides, the research says it's what people want to hear."

"Okay, then 'H$_2$O: The Wetter Water.'"

I stepped into Lionel's field of vision. "I don't mean to change the subject, but over on Water Street there's a kind of situation developing that you might like to know about."

An aide swept all the photos to the floor. "Why even advertise H$_2$O? Anything we say could backfire. Tap doesn't advertise. It's like oxygen and paved streets. H$_2$O is a given."

"Maybe that's our campaign."

"Advertise by not advertising."

"No, but in our ads we tell people that this isn't something you advertise."

The Director waved me away. "Don't tell me about the amnesia. People's memories actually improved once we replaced their water with H$_2$O."

"Yes, but this is something else. H$_2$O has a secondary property that could prove quite dangerous, and until I can refute a certain dire theory, I'm going to continue to believe the worst."

"Maybe that's your problem."

"The process is flawed," I said. "But I'm overseeing the development of a patch."

"Now you're overseeing. Impressive."

"It will be simple and inexpensive, but it will mean a decrease in output. I assure you, it will be kept to a minimum.

Julian appeared, replacing the mayor's drink. "What would you say about a man who purchased a temporary wife?"

"Temporary? A technological breakthrough!"

It was like a sock in the gut. I swallowed hard and tried again to reach the Director. "Do you know what could happen if H_2O passes through those filters for a second time?"

One of the creatives proclaimed: "H_2Flow."

"Julian, help these people," said Lionel.

"Here's how I view the hydrocrisis," Julian began. "It's divorce, on a molecular scale. Hydrogen and oxygen no longer see eye to eye, but we're all hoping for reconciliation, so we bring them together in a controlled, moderated setting. I don't have to tell you it's not the same as before, but we live in the future, right? We're used to that." There was something bakery fresh about the mixed scent of perspiration and hair oil that came off of him. We were all entranced by the double scoop of a man leaning back on barstool and his romantic vision of two (three, actually) estranged atoms making googly eyes at each other after a harsh separation. The best lawyers are always seducers, capable of becoming beautiful and desirable at will, no matter how ugly.

"Now, once we have them back together, how do we make it stick? Do we use threats and intimidation? Do we assign blame and compel obedience? Sure it would feel good. Those two really have it coming. But we're not interested in revenge. Haven't we had enough revenge for one century? Let's focus on results. We want these two crazy atoms to fall in love with each other all over again. That's what the filter does. It's a love charm, an aphrodisiac, cupid's arrow."

"Okay, I got it: 'Hydrogen and Oxygen: A Lifelong Bond.'"

The oleaginous marketing director leaned in to me. "Our margins are extremely tight as it is." He gestured towards the table. "Selling this stuff isn't cheap. Community outreach costs money, government relations, mandatory capital improvements, insurance, compliance, risk avoidance. These are the burdens we shoulder. We don't proceed with a project of this magnitude without approvals from three different auditing firms. It's a bit late to recalibrate an undertaking upon which so much has already been staked. We'd require more time, and more to go on than vague warnings from a dark-horse candidate for Chief Engineer."

That last phrase stung more than it should have, but then Lionel came to my side and said, "Can we shoulder a new expense on the eve of the launch? Can we withstand a decrease in output?" He paused, and nobody in the room dared guess the answer. "No doubt about it," he laughed, "if it means safe drinking water for the people of Chicago. That's our business!"

Everybody laughed with him, and I sketched the patch, as well as I could understand it, on the back of an envelope. There was plenty of blank paper in the room, but one of the creatives suggested the envelope because that's where innovative solutions are supposed to arise. It would be photographed immediately and included in the press package.

I left the Snows the way I'd entered, noting with curiosity the squish under my shoes with each step along the red carpet but not wanting to investigate. There was a leak somewhere, that's all, a real leak from a fake fountain but never mind. I boarded the inbound train, an old Amtrak double-decker crowded with casino amateurs.

I believe that my next steps remain defensible, even in light of my admittedly overprotective feelings toward my invention, my baby monster who was now grown up and ready to go out into the world to wreak who knows what havoc. The Drixa Corporation had grown too big, too arrogant, and too slow to babysit. That role rightly belonged to a different kind of entity, more sensitive to the monster's temper.

Chapter Sixteen

Rain had begun falling from an animé sky by the time we pulled into Union Station. Thousands of tiny fists of water massaged the windows, testing their strength. I strained to decode the pattern of the rivulets, trying to decide whether to get off downtown or to see where Amtrak would take me next—Kankakee or Rockford, a bungalow somewhere complete with a basement in which Yemina and I could continue experimenting until the risks and potential of H_2O were better understood. Hayden Jr. could visit one weekend a month and maybe stay for all of July. We could all walk into town together each morning and eat a big breakfast in the diner before heading over to the river for some fishing or to the baseball diamond to watch one church against another. By the fourth inning, Yemina would catch onto the basics of the game. The boy would meticulously fill out his scorecard and theatrically boo the ump for calling strikes when they were high and outside.

My reverie was interrupted by a gap-toothed conductor. "Last shtop, Union Shtation. Did you bring an umbrella, shir? Better shee if they have one in the shtore." The station was nearly empty, and the store was out of umbrellas, so I bought a rain bonnet instead, and a *Tribune*, and I felt proud not to feel too proud to tuck the latter under my arm and to fold the former into a triangle and tie the ends under my chin as I climbed the slick marble stairs and entered the downpour.

The rain bombed down on me, leaving dents in the bonnet. Adams Street was clogged with cars that I easily outpaced by foot.

The wind had picked up, and trees that had weathered more than one storm-of-the-century swayed and creaked. Electricity tuning-forked the sky, and a low whistle filled the silences between the drops, the sound of a colossal body streaking through the atmosphere. Nearly human shapes slouched through slanted alleys. Huddled bunches hatched botched plots in the half-light. Every stride brought me closer to Water Street and the purportedly harmless brew stored in those glass-lined vats.

True, ICE-9 had languished for too long as the loyal opposition, but they were my only hope. They had been subdued by their freedom to communicate whatever message they wanted, which made them oblivious to its failure to dent Drixa propaganda. Sarcastic handouts and witty T-shirts wouldn't cut it anymore. Something new was needed, something to jolt them out of their diverting but complacent street theater. Something that would turn the lapdog into a pit bull. Well, it was in my pocket and it wasn't doing me any good. Divorce proceedings had robbed me of the power to own anything outright, but their hands weren't tied.

I would mix ammonia and bleach, so to speak, and await the reaction. Nearing the plant, I heard waves slapping the embankment along Lake Shore Drive, drenching the traffic and carrying away antennae and license plates in the breakers. Then all at once, the rain stopped, and the street looked back at me.

I found Aqua at the mouth of a tunnel, emerging from behind a door improvised from corrugated metal and particleboard. "What a coincidence, we were just writing you a letter. Actually we finished about an hour ago."

"Can I see?"

"It's an *open* letter. You can read it in the paper tomorrow, but I'll give you a hint. It doesn't contain the word *martyr*."

"What about *traitor, fool, sucker*?"

"Getting warmer."

"Aw c'mon. I may be a fool, but I'm no sucker. Aren't we talking right now?"

"Not yet."

"H_2O doesn't cause amnesia," I told her.

"H_2O is a fake," she answered. "You just figured it out. The stuff he's launching isn't really fake water, it's real water labeled as fake."

"Fake fake water."

"He knows we're planning something big, and he thinks he knows how to absorb my hardest hit. ICE-9 blocks the fake H_2O and it goes away for eight, ten months only to come back as new and improved H_2O."

"And ICE-9 beats them again."

"Only this time, nobody listens. They think, *Hey, Drixa fixed all that. This stuff is safe now and those protestors are still shouting the same old tired slogans.* They think, *pass the H_2O, I'm thirsty.* ICE-9 beats themselves."

"The New Coke gambit," I assented. "Public demand for the familiar product is stronger than ever. Extortionary prices will be paid just to hold onto the same old stuff."

"On the other hand, if ICE-9 acquiesces, they're stuck selling real water as fake from now on."

"So you're saying we should just lie back and let it happen?" When I spoke to her there was a crackling in my ears like radio static or the wrapper of a starlight mint. She must have gotten that all the time. To beautiful women, men are just a little distracted, that's all.

"H_2O doesn't exist yet, don't you see? But eight months from now, it's anyone's guess."

"Or ten," I agreed. "One more thing . . ."

This was it. The watch said 11:58. That's the hour and minute my career committed suicide, the fateful action that tagged me as just another loser on the ladder, distracted by pretty eyes and pretty talk. The night air felt close and saturated. The sound of a diesel engine was heard, and soon an off-duty ambulance lumbered up to us, piloted by the kid with the anorak.

I removed a document from my pocket.

"Here, let me use your back," I said. She turned around and let me add my signature to the document."

"What's this?"

"It's yours now."

She squinted in the moonglow. "It looks like an agenda for the kickoff."

"Oh, wait. Wrong piece of paper. Here."

I agree that any and all patents, awards, royalties, and reimbursements proceeding from my work as a Drixa employee belong to Annabelle Dawson in perpetuity.

I signed the letter, and she took it from me and turned without a word and then ran around to the rear doors of the ambulance. Good-bye, promotion.

I envisioned Aqua strutting past the guards at Drixa headquarters. Anyone who challenges her is met with a confident wink, but no explanation is tendered until she is escorted up the elevator and into her father's office. Lionel Dawson is pleased to see her; he waves away the security and invites her to have a seat. He offers (and she accepts) a glass of vintage water and compliments her healthy appearance. He praise her for taking the first step toward reconciliation, emphasizing how much he'd like to put their differences behind them. She says little, waiting for him to fall silent. Maybe she lets him squirm for a minute before showing him what she's carrying in a small leather briefcase that she got as a high school graduation gift from him.

There I stood—Hayden Shivers, drink fink. This was the river whose course had been reversed. The city had taken action to keep sewage out of the drinking water. More than a hundred years later, a corporation was subtracting water from the water.

Chicago was swaddled in its blanket of snow and good fortune. Whatever evils had been perpetrated by Drixa in the name of profit, they paled beside the hazards of fortune that had plunged two-thirds of the globe into crisis—a multitude of crises, actually, one overlapping the next, environmental and economic, inevitable and unpredictable, fires, earthquakes, plagues, clashes, agitations, and assassinations in countries whose names I had never heard previously but whose geopolitical significance was never thereafter doubted.

After a while you don't feel lucky anymore; you feel overdue. The bell was tolling for Chicago. Something strong was headed straight for it, something powerful enough to break its big shoulders.

Soaking wet, freezing cold, I stumbled back to the Brahms, feeling like a prizefighter who just climbed back into the ring after a decade in retirement. At first the old moves were returning but then I got carried away. I wanted to lie down someplace dark, or eat a bowl of ice cream, or listen to soothing, familiar music. Better yet, all three.

Although I hadn't technically left Chicago, my trip to Las Vegas had opened my eyes to Chicago's vast and fissured dignity. You have to move about to appreciate a city. Prisoners and patients can't be said to reside at the addresses where the jails and hospitals are located. And nobody so fully inhabits a city as its homeless.

I silently reviewed my talking points for my last chance to set the record straight. Outlining your thoughts before speaking can and should be difficult. Every bullet point invites ten digressions, and before you know it you're embroidering pleasures and shames quite remote from your objectives.

I thought I'd begin by praising Drixa for creating an environment where innovations such as H_2O were possible. That would strike a suitably modest note. I'd also extol ICE-9's forbearance in working with rather than against the target of their protest. Once I'd made it clear that I wasn't about to take sole credit for the invention, I'd underscore the wide-ranging benefits of a synthetic, waterlike substance. The list of domestic, industrial, and agricultural applications could go on for pages, and the gains in safety far outweighed the potential side effects. A few instances of amnesia and delusion amounted to statistical insignificance compared to the widespread death resulting from widespread drought and continental water-borne disease. Wasn't it true, I'd half-joke, that we all to some extent forget the past anyway and construct the present every single day of our lives?

Who was I kidding? The heart of Drixa's communication strategy was the indefatigable faith possessing every last person on the payroll. By expunging dissent and disgruntlement and purging whistleblowers and rotten apples before they could do harm, the HR department made the PR department obsolete. "Drixa's big secret? Dedication to pure water from Lionel on down," was all Warne Shoals or any other reporter could get out of anyone. Despite the degraded parody of water issuing from Chicago's taps, purity was still the byword. Of course, compared to what most of the world was forced to drink, Drixa could rightly claim to be providing a fresh and healthy service, but after a certain point, relativism strips definitions from words like hurricanes strip bark from trees. Trees cannot survive without bark.

By welcoming the most ardent eco-activists under the Drixa umbrella, Miyumi Park had successfully co-opted even their venomous agenda. I reminded myself to be careful with her, but our strategic powers were so mismatched that there was no point in worrying about it. As a Drixa employee, no matter what I said would sound like an endorsement.

The Brahms lobby was empty. Not just empty of guests, but completely empty. As in completely. Silent and smokeless, with no trace of earlier events. And something had ozonized the air, clarifying it and improving breathability.

I really wanted a snack. Hotels put out buffets with chafing dishes full of pancakes or ribs or whatever, right? Especially with such foul weather outside. The Pepper Mill couldn't accommodate everybody, but more tables could be set up in the lobby. Guests wouldn't soon forget such a conscientious gesture. Luther Brahms (1871–1917) would be proud.

In the Pepper Mill, a black woman sat facing her can of lemonade. To avoid detection by ICE-9, Yemina was in costume, a rented uniform of indecipherable purpose, somewhere between security guard and flight attendant. Her hair was bunned and glasses tinted to maximize anonymity, but upon closer scrutiny, there was something new in her face that had nothing to do with disguise. Her forehead burned with an awful premonition, and her skin had gone ashen. I used to reflect on how lucky she was to have escaped her life in Africa and even took some credit for her good fortune, but her fate must not have been as rosy as my self-congratulation indicated. Or maybe her life in Africa would have had its own travails.

"I recommend the chicken," I said. She didn't reply. "The tagging mechanism," I said. "They're going to adopt it right away."

"You went to see Lionel?"

"He's receptive to the safeguards we discussed. I gave them the patch."

"What does that mean? You gave them the patch." I'd never seen her so agitated.

"That's what I call the method you outlined for filtering out the H_2O before it reaches the filter."

"Yes, but in your 'patch,' what detects the H_2O? Hayden, I've tried everything, and nothing but the fungus itself reacts differently to water than to H_2O."

"Of course," I said. "The fungus. That's what we're talking about."

She fell silent for a moment. "We thought we were making life, but it was death in disguise."

"It's just like you said. If we tag each new molecule, they can be centrifuged out before hitting the water main."

"Let me ask you this, and I don't mean rhetorically. How does your patch let the H_2O come in contact with the fungus without even more being produced?"

Chapter Seventeen

In haste, I returned to the tunnel to see whether Aqua had fared any better with Lionel than I had. The anorak-wearing protestor emerged from the doorway. There were others beside him, shrouded and heaving. The wind, Chicago's celebrated spirit, etched parallel lines along our anatomies. It was a city of plastic combs, a place where you had to speak up.

"Where's the girl?" one said.

"The last time I saw her, she was getting into an ambulance with you," I said.

"Don't be foolish," he swallowed.

"It's okay, I worked it out with Aqua. See? The launch is going to be fine. They're going to blame you for my fall. 'HS Down. 2:46.' That's me. I stole this from payroll. They've got it all planned out. MoC, that's Mayor of Chicago, get it?" I was hoping not to have to explain what my signature was doing at the bottom of the document.

They all spun around, and I followed them inside. We passed through the cobwebbed dankness of the tunnel and soon emerged in a blindingly pristine space, a room large enough to accommodate three long white sofas and an array of tables and chairs in coordinated minimalist styles. Recessed lights gave the illusion of sunlight through rice paper, though we were two or more stories below ground.

I couldn't discern the purpose of the room or determine whether the protestors had constructed it themselves or coopted an existing space for an alternate use. A bank of video monitors displayed the Brahms lobby, the courtyard of the Justice complex, and the interior of the Drixa plant.

"Welcome to the Snowflake Lodge," my host said, throwing off his covering to reveal a frail, courtly frame and delicate features.

"Elegant," I replied.

"We think so. Many of our visitors expect alpine décor, like a ski lodge, but the name snowflake comes from the color of the walls, of course, as well as the geometric pattern formed by the corridors."

"Where are the girls?" I asked.

"Are you looking for a replacement?"

"Perhaps."

"With your history, that may be difficult," he smiled. "But of course you are a special case. Why don't you wait here, and I'll see if Varuk will see you."

A frosted vitrine running along one wall held rows of stoppered vials.

2014 Southern Africa
2011 The Caribbean
2005 New Orleans, Louisiana
2004 Aceh, Indonesia
1999 Venezuela
1977 Johnstown, PA
1970 Bangladesh
1953 Iran
1889 Johnstown, PA
1887 Huayan Kou, China
1228 Holland

The liquid was a slightly different color in each vial, but, generally, the older the flood, the darker. In some, a layer of sediment had collected. Sometimes algae coated the glass. As Varuk approached, I caught a whiff of something floral.

"Where's Yemina?" he asked.

"Where's Aqua?" I responded.

"This now, the real ICE-9. The anarchism. We are hating this . . . compromise and . . . conciliation." His mouth was wetter than I would have liked it to be. "We still respecting what you trying do," he turned to me. "Or else you wouldn't be alive."

"Thank you."

"You always are inventor H_2O. You always . . . rebalance table of elements."

"It could help a lot of people."

"It is too genius! Crush some . . . fungus with mortar and pestle, spread it to the filter, turn on the water, and . . . Yin no more fitting Yang."

"Thanks, but."

"Where the girl?"

"How would I know? She left me."

"Wait, there she is!" a voice gasped behind us.

"Huh?"

"Aqua, there, on TV. She's standing beside her father on TV."

"Oh," I said. "Oh fuck."

There on the screen, the director and his daughter stood in front of a banner that said: **The Water of the Future.** Lionel had profited from the most advanced media instruction available. In person, he could come off as distant, heartless, but in front of a camera he radiated authority. He made his better self available, forged intimate ties with his unseen audience, uttered platitudes as though they had dawned upon him after long years of study and meditation.

Wondrous as a seller and miraculous as a motivational speaker, he had reached his apotheosis as director. The staff revered him, quoted his speeches to their children, and scoffed at the suggestion in the *Tribune* that he might have the political muscle to unseat Mayor King: why would he settle for mayor? Even the protestors admired his panache. His farewell speech was set to generate headlines of a size normally reserved for events of the most historic significance.

Aqua Bella was corporately outfitted and newly coiffured. In person, she had poise enough to stun me like beautiful music played on a dog whistle. The face that appeared on the video monitor, however, was not the same. Her features had an almost teenaged upsweep, as though gravity hadn't started working yet. Her complexion was oily, her posture imperfect. You could hear her breath on the microphone, the pop of her lips opening.

I was drawn and repelled, drawn and repelled, the attraction and repulsion each stronger for the existence of the other. Consequently, not everything that Lionel and Aqua Bella said in their introductory remarks registered. Was this press conference taking place inside the plant? The brick walls did not appear onscreen, but their acoustic effect was palpable. This machinery normally operated at a deafening volume, and since the attendants' voices were clear, I reasoned that the plant was down. The logic pleased me, and I rehearsed it over in my mind for sheer enjoyment, but soon the flow of thought overran the low walls of this one subject, stimulating a rude sequence of questions and anxieties.

Thinking of everything at once wasn't possible, let alone keeping track of how it all related, but the *more* you could think of, the more accurate a mental picture you could form, which gave you the advantage in the next round. (There was always a next round, right?)

"*Protestor named Director*! Nobody's going to believe it!"

"Just tell me that Drixa under the daughter will be a bit less mysterious, more transparent than Drixa under the father."

"Of course I pledge absolute transparency, especially in our international dealings. Transparency in all things! We're a water company, after all."

She instinctively knew to banter with her admirers and not to commit to a specific course of action.

"Tell me I've drunk my last can of Country Life."

"Oh, I don't know," she drawled. "I'm starting to like it."

"But that aluminum taste—ugh!"

"You poor thing, did you forget to open the can?" It wasn't part of a routine. She herself was the routine.

Lionel took the mike to conclude the press conference and summarized, "The launch of our new H_2O service will go on as scheduled. See you all at the Millennium Park tomorrow at noon. Effective immediately, Ms. Dawson assumes leadership of Drixa International and the title of Director, while . . . " He paused to let a winning smile spread over his face, "while her father hits the showers." On cue, the plant roared to life, turbines accelerating and pistons pulsating in taut harmony, which quickly rose to a deafening, painful volume.

To me, the scene on the monitor felt less like a current event than an archived fact of history, no longer relevant, but Varuk lunged at the set and pulled it to the ground. The act did not have the dramatic effect that he had envisioned, nor did kicking the dead screen for emphasis.

"What you think? You no behave responsibility? You want me no behave responsibility? You want we declaring amnesty on lost African wives?"

"I'm as concerned as you are," I said. "My lawyer is right this moment looking for her . . . Not him personally, but—"

With the excess strength that was left in his muscles after the monitor had toppled easier than expected, he took me by the throat. Upon meeting my eyes, however, he relaxed his grip. "You find before launch. Yes?"

Varuk's hair smelled like orange blossom. I rose dizzily and stutter-stepped down a hallway toward a stairwell. The metal steps chimed out with surprisingly gorgeous carillon music as I half-fell up them.

It was a mistake to think that a job well done guaranteed anything. If anything, it just got you into deeper trouble. Everyone eventually wants to try what they'll fail at, and the same goes for corporations, nations, civilizations. Take Drixa, for instance.

Had Lionel Dawson rushed H_2O to market before it was ready? Did the company fully cooperate with the Independent Council on the Environment? I didn't know what went wrong, just that trouble began when a man and his company went beyond their competency.

The protestors, too, had also overextended themselves. Never a monolithic movement in the first place, ICE-9 splintered dramatically as H_2O's promise came true. Some activists threw in the towel, reasoning that pure water—the holy grail of the organization— would now be plentiful and accessible. Others grew more militant; dismayed at their defecting brethren, they pointed to Drixa's long history of manipulation and evasion and resolved to cut all ties with the corporation as the first step on a path toward all-out war. Still others maintained that open communication with Drixa continued to be the best way to get their concerns heard. Miyumi held regular sessions with this last contingent, but suspicious of spies and saboteurs, she slipped in the odd bit of misinformation ("desalinization technologies are endangering lives the world over"), a precaution that further alienated the potentially sympathetic. Further, she insisted that ICE-9 sever its ties with the Snowflake Lodge before relations were normalized. Her offer to make up for the shortfall was met with considerable indignation and left the organization grasping for alternative revenue streams, including the services of the Snowflake Lodge.

Yemina's quest for knowledge had come into conflict with her respect for secrets. The difference between water and H_2O was a secret the fungus knew, and like any secret it was sacred.

And what about me? What was my big mistake? When I went from building filters to building molecules, maybe? Could be.

CHAPTER EIGHTEEN

Source: Maltese Making Own H_2O
By Warne Shoals

Despite extensive precautions, the recipe for manufacture of H_2O has fallen into the hands of the tiny Mediterranean republic of Malta, according to intelligence officials, and production of the waterlike substance is under way. In a report issued late last week and anonymously mailed to this reporter from an address inside the Justice Complex, a Maltese laboratory with international backing is said to be producing and distributing H_2O throughout the region. Drixa, the leading and until now the only H_2O producer in the world, has refused to comment on the development, but analysts warn of market destabilization and potentially dire consequences for the agriculture, travel, and utilities industries.

In a related matter, citing the sensitive nature of the ongoing investigation, officials refused to comment on the recent arrest of Ginelle Shivers, a local woman from a prominent Kenwood family but with known Maltese associations.

The news rushed into my bloodstream like a radiological dye exposing cancer.

News had reached the island of an invention that required the fungus to operate, but rumors were agitating the populace rather than guaranteeing future wealth. One report held that a U.S. army freighter was set to tow Fungus Rock away under cover of night, and so a blockade of fishing boats was marshaled whose round-the-clock vigil fell apart after thirty-six hours. Another story circulated that Sicily had declared Fungus Rock its dominion and that negotiations were under way that would cut Malta out of the deal. The value of Maltese fungus on the futures market fluctuated wildly and was just above gold on the day Ginelle arrived to search for her mother.

"Welcome, Chicago!" said the driver.

"This is my second visit." The long flight had left her weak, with a painful knot in the exact center of her skull. Her jaw felt mis-aligned, and it hurt to say ems and ens.

"There are many opportunities here. So many!"

"I see the airport has expanded. When I was here seven years ago it was just a hangar and a landing strip."

"Seven years, might as well have been a hundred years. Your company must have high hopes for Malta and what Malta has to offer. I'm a man of peace, but if it's bombs that are making us pros-per, Chicago, I say *bombs away*!"

"But I'm not here for bombs."

"Bombs away, Miss Chicago, here's your hotel."

Later, in a windowless hotel bar, a few elderly German couples presided solemnly over used glasses of beer. Nobody turned to look when the door opened and lemony Maltese sunlight wedged onto whitewashed floorboards. She hesitated in the doorway before taking a seat at the bar without removing headscarf or sunglasses.

She wished she could postpone her appointment another day, but she lacked both phone number and phone. Hypersensitivity to cigarette smoke didn't count in this country, let alone this bar with-out windows—more prison cell than bar—where the smoke turned extra carcinogenic when it finally came in contact with sunlight.

She blinked in vain for tears to bathe her tired eyes. A lot was wrong with her: circulation sluggish, respiration shallow, orientation skewed. On the flight from London the airlines had served a fish pie that she bit into thinking it was going to be dessert, and she could still taste the fish oil on her swollen tongue and parched tonsils. She wanted to cough but could not. She wanted to go home, to be home with her little boy.

"Missus Shivers."

A man behind her leaned hard against the bar, and when she turned to him the pain in her head flared up. "Please," she answered. "Have a seat."

"*Tanks* but if I am sitting I not can get up. Old men. Missus Shivers I am so happy to meet you. You are even more lovely than I imagined. The resemblance is striking."

"People say he looks like Hayden."

"Pardon?"

"Never mind, I misunderstood."

The encounters between Ginelle and Tomas, a name I didn't learn until later, absorb me like scenes from a movie discovered on late-night television, halfway over. The momentum is palpable, the action thrilling despite its obscurity. Everyone has something at stake, and you take it for granted that it's worthwhile. The set-up is more convincing, being obscure.

"If you please we can begin tomorrow morning. I have plenty photographs and letters. I am working for you these many days. Your husband will be joining us?"

"No, just me. My husband's very busy at work just now and couldn't travel."

"Work is very important in America."

"Yes, well, he wants to be Chief Engineer at Drixa, which is a big c—"

"Yes, I know Drixa."

"About tomorrow . . . do you live here in Rabat?"

"Not here, but close by in San Lawrenz near the Fungus Rock." He saw how the name stung her eyes. "You know it? Funny name, it's okay to laugh."

"Do you know where I can buy sunblock? I don't think I can go out there again without something to protect my skin."

Thanks to a utility conglomerate in a place called Chicago, the Maltese economy had caught up to the twenty-first century in a few short months. Arabic speculators and Australian entrepreneurs flocked to the markets, luring small children from tables laden with glass and lace to serve as translators on deals for oceanfront property, motorboats, and government bonds. Ginelle had difficulty finding a hotel room, settling finally on partitioned space in a hastily converted barracks.

Her headache would not abate, and she spent the time she had between meetings in the darkest, quietest places she could find, usually old churches built on the site of saintly visitations. Perhaps owing to the sudden frenzy of promised economic prosperity, nobody noticed her enough to remark on her resemblance to anyone.

Lemony light stinging like lemon juice in her eyes, Ginelle waited for her guide, worried that the arrangements weren't clear enough. A statue of the Virgin eyed her from a scalloped shrine. Maybe this was the wrong corner. Maybe he was waiting for her back in the hotel bar. Why had they never discussed precisely what he'd be doing for her, how long it would take, how much it would cost?

Hayden Shivers was a character in this film without ever appearing onscreen. My presence was felt as the harsh light, the ache in her head. During the previous visit, at the tail end of an overlong, unfortunate honeymoon slash research expedition, I had sought this place out. What was up? It was a hunch, I'd shrugged with a secretiveness Ginelle didn't recognize. Normally I tried too hard to impress her with engineering, but when it came to this new hobby, I kept mum—embarrassed by the scale of the aspiration. The secrecy made her curious, but when she'd descended the basement stairs she hadn't known what she was looking for.

Ginelle found the guide leaning against a barrel on the wharf, watching two seagulls tearing open a fat sea bass on the edge of the sand, liberating a slender green fish from inside the larger fish's belly.

He didn't react as if she were late, or early, or as if this was or was not the intended meeting place. She went along with it, this pretense that they had run into each other quite by accident, a couple of friendly acquaintances, and followed him to a concrete slab shaded by a tin-roofed shack.

His cock-eyed necktie reminded her of Julian. In fact, there was so much of Julian in this Maltese "guide"—the jowls, the big expressionless hands like mittens, the tendency to lean against any available wall—whom Julian (through an associate) had found for her that she fleetingly imagined herself to be speaking to the lawyer in disguise.

He produced a small brown jar for her inspection.

"Oh, no, thank you, but that's suntan oil. I was looking for sunblock." He shrugged as if it were a semantic question, or a brand preference. "Should I have brought my own papers?" she asked, pointing at the manila file in his mitts.

"If you think they help. As you wish. Some people think it's good to show all of it, others want privacy, as they wish."

"You must get sent many clients like me."

"No," he smiled, almost charmingly. "Nobody like you."

His file was filled with bad xeroxes of old photos, and he showed these one by one, pointing out the relevant women when there might be some doubt.

Some had her eyebrows. Others had her posture. One woman in a black coat smiled like Ginelle, but her stout ankles didn't correspond with the recollections of the women in the market.

The last image in the stack quickened her pulse. The thin, tallish figure in the church doorway had heavy eyebrows and a flat nose just like hers. Standing proud, looking scrubbed and serene.

But—oh!—there was something not quite right about this picture. Ginelle tried not to betray her doubts. She just handed the file back, not mentioning that the woman in a pictured dated thirty years earlier was wearing the seed pearl necklace that I had given her seven years ago.

147

Then all at once she knew what this man was really after. "These pictures are so very interesting," she swallowed.

"I have many more."

"We'll have to meet again. If you're free for lunch tomorrow . . . I'd like to tell you about my husband's work, his research."

"As you wish," he confirmed, drawing meaning out of the three words like raw meat from a beached creature.

Ginelle knew what she wanted but not whether the agent had what she wanted, and vice versa. If they didn't want what they wanted as much as they wanted it, they wouldn't have gone on like this. Their complementary demands drove them together. If they had it, they could simply give each other what they wanted, but the uncertainty of the other's having it kept each of them as shrewd as scalpels.

The third meeting took place in her hotel room. This time, recognizing his weak hand in the Missing Persons department, he took a different tack. "The islanders have given up hope. They are ready to be annexed by Italy, Spain, England . . . "

"No!"

"Yes, they are ready to surrender the remaining tatters of their once-proud culture. It's only a matter of time before the ground beneath us sold, hectare by hectare, at a price too low to even insult us. To have the fungus but not the technology to capitalize on it is the final bad joke at our expense."

Juiced by their standoff, the agent and the orphan, he forgetting duty sworn to his country, she forgetting her repulsion, consummate their betrayal one afternoon against a rusted-out, empty bathtub.

Afterwards, on hands and knees, she crawls to her suitcase and unlocks the lock. From inside, she removes a poorly assembled handheld device that she has swiped from her husband's lab.

Only the thought that Ginelle's sin arguably bested mine assuaged my indignation.

Fade to black.

Chapter Nineteen

When you take a pin and prick a balloon filled with water, it might start to dribble or it might burst, but either way it's the pin's fault. Similarly, there is no such thing as an unintentional betrayal, but the severity of the consequences varies independently of the depth of betrayal.

Ginelle's betrayal of me was partly a response to my betrayal of her, and you might say we both stuck our pins in the same balloon, a determined, curious Zambian refugee of nineteen.

Yemina's parents were dead, and so were all but three of her nine brothers and sisters—as far as she knew. I hadn't bothered to find out any more background than that. She had charisma, and strangers always wanted to confide in her and to protect her. She was lucky to be like that, and it took an additional dose of luck to get her to Chicago just weeks before an earthquake devastated her country.

There was nothing to be ashamed of in the way I treated her. That is, except for hiring her in the first place, which was more like hiring a car than hiring an employee, let alone a wife and collaborator. The fact that our unnatural arrangement felt natural attested more to her personal charm than to any virtue I might claim.

This same charm must have been operating at full force when Ginelle came home from her Maltese failure to find her son playing the game of Sorry! with a stranger who had obviously come to feel right at home. There she was at the table, absorbed in strategy, half-eaten fishstick and a half-drunk glass of milk pushed to one side. I cringed at the thought of the scene but went on picturing it, trying to imagine what Yemina had said that convinced Ginelle to let her stay. To kick out the creep instead.

Maybe it would have been better if I had avoided women altogether. The interactions were permanently corrupt. More than any particular quality, it was the subtle differences between them that attracted me—Aqua Bella's smarts versus Yemina's brilliance; Ginelle's patriotism as opposed to Miyumi's loyalty—but my ambition to please and impress remained constant. Every move was calibrated toward winning trust, not to exploit it, but to have it for its own sake, which wasn't much better.

It was time to check out of the room. As I dressed for the launch, the consequences of this habit lay spread out before me like the toxic contents of the once-great lake. Every shirt on the bed had been given to me by a woman.

My resolve to avoid them already evaporated, I dialed a number on the phone. "I'm glad it's you," said the voice on the other end.

"Aqua, the Brahms c—"

"Annabelle," she corrected. "Annabelle Dawson, Director of Drixa Enterprises Worldwide."

"The whole city could go under."

"Now where have I heard that before?"

"But—"

"It's different this time," she finished for me.

"It is different this time."

"Every five years or so, somebody starts another sky-is-falling crusade, running to Warne Shoals and raising a frenzy about the city going under, and you know what happens? Nothing. The city endures another five years, long enough to breed the next wave of hysterics and the next."

"Once you start the H_2O," I said, "there may not be a way to shut it off."

"Members of our unparalleled team of engineers will be available at the launch to answer all your questions," she answered in a tone that would not permit a follow-up question.

Unconsoled, I punched in another number. Miyumi Park certainly wouldn't approve of the new Drixa team unless it included her. As Human Resources Manager, she reserved certain rights. She was no longer a loyal employee but the sine qua non. "Just verifying we are good for the kickoff," I said. "When does the shit come down?"

"The hill has been captured, the prisoners are tied up, and brass band is rehearsing. We just need you to plant the flag while we snap pictures."

"What kind of turnout are they expecting?"

"Couple thousand. Some people come for the free samples. Some see a crowd and join it because they don't want to miss anything. You nervous?"

"I just want to know what to expect."

"It'll be just like rehearsal except real. That's what rehearsal means."

"Good, good, good," I said. "But the dive, let's just focus on that dive one more minute here. Shouldn't the ceremonial first sip go down smooth? I was thinking about going with a smile and wave instead of the whole falling thing. How does that sound?"

"Where's the excitement in that?"

"This is a ceremony," I protested. "There's not supposed to be excitement. Usually rehearsals are to make sure nothing happens at the real thing."

"Well if you want the dive to be real . . . " I heard blood on the phone. "I think I can straighten this out. You just have to picture the whole thing on a television screen. A man sips this billion dollar miracle and falls down dead."

"Dead?"

"Presumably dead, yes. Less than a hundred feet away stands a group of anarchists and saboteurs."

"Protestors."

"Exactly, and the anarchists are out to destroy Drixa and its new life-saving product. Who gets the blame? The widely respected corporate citizen with everything to gain by filtering all the excitement out of the kickoff? Or the—"

"Protestors."

"Exactly."

"Does a hearse come and get me?" I asked.

"An ambulance," Miyumi corrected. "Victims aren't pronounced dead on the scene unless decapitated or disemboweled. The ambulance belongs to us. The paramedics are on our payroll."

"How long does it all take?"

"You're on the ground for one solid minute. That may not seem like a long time now, but it's going to feel like an eternity. You may start wondering whether the plan went awry, but rest assured the paramedics are on their way. After sixty seconds have elapsed, you're loaded into the vehicle. Thirty seconds more and you're gone from the scene."

"What happens at the hospital?"

"There's no hospital. You're not injured, remember? Unless . . ."

"No," I said. "No injuries, I'm fine."

"The ambulance takes you to a house in the suburbs where the next phase begins." I listened to the details of the funeral.

"It will be an intimate affair, invitation only, but also televised," Miyumi began. "Hayden Shivers' life, edited into video clips that emphasize his many years of public service and devotion to family. It all leads up to the moment he accepted the Drixa commission, a turning point the pundits will respectfully debate. On one hand, you have the promising career, the idealistic goals sacrificed on the altar of corporate greed. On the other, you have the dedication and vision that must be honored out of respect for the dead. Footage of him sipping the H_2O and collapsing will replay endlessly. A few bad jokes will circulate on talk radio and the Internet. These have been shown to accelerate martyrdom and inspire public sentiment. Hayden Shivers walks into a bar."

"Pardon?"

"You never heard this? Hayden Shivers walks into a bar. 'Sorry,' says the bartender. 'The floor's kind of sticky.'"

"I'm not sure I—"

"Wait, have you heard this one? What's the difference between Hayden Shivers and a soufflé?"

"Okay, I give up."

"When a soufflé falls, it's not the soufflé's fault."

"I have a joke," I said. "What is Hayden Shivers's favorite time of year?"

"What?"

"The fall."

"That's a good one. Really, good. I'll have to remember that one."

"What did Hayden Shivers and William Faulkner have in common?" I continued. "They both had drinking problems."

"That's good too, but it needs work. I'll shop it around the office and see if anyone can polish it up. Drinking problem is good, but there might be a better drunk than Faulkner. And Hayden? White shirt, please."

With hardly a thought for how she knew I had been buttoning a blue shirt at that moment, I followed her instruction and went down to the lobby.

CHAPTER TWENTY

Pierre Amu Lucluc steered the car through medium traffic. Miyumi left me to my thoughts, which strayed from subject to subject without finding a purchase.

I knew the actions I was to perform but not what they meant. Theories suggested themselves but did not survive scrutiny. One minute I'd be trying to see myself through the eyes of a faceless corporation—the eternal *why me?*—the next I'd be wondering who would tune in—the eternal *why not me?*

Warne Shoals called. "I got something for the fact-checking department."

"Shoot," I said.

Company Acknowledges That H_2O Self-Generates
By Warne Shoals
A representative for Drixa, the water concern, confirmed today that under certain circumstances, their synthetic water product "grows," but he insisted that the growth was far less than the .1% per month that opponents allege. Reports of the process, known as "reverse evaporation," surfaced earlier this week but were initially disputed by the company.

"In ordinary conditions, H_2O behaves exactly like your ordinary tapwater," explained the source. "However, we acknowledge the validity and legitimacy of laboratory tests showing that our product can be made to behave abnormally when subjected to abnormal conditions." Saying that such information was a trade secret, and indeed a matter of national security, he declined to elaborate on the exact conditions necessary.

ICE-9, the most prominent of the activist groups questioning H_2O's safety, hailed the announcement as a victory but criticized the company for its lack of frankness and underestimation of the potential consequences of reverse evaporation, a process they dub mushrooming. "Just imagine what could happen once they pump out enough of this stuff," Varuk Prechand stated. "Can you? Neither can I. Neither can Drixa. All we're asking for is further testing before H_2O is fully unleashed." Prechand went on to emphasize ICE-9's position that the severity of the hydrocrisis demanded swift—but not reckless—action.

Prechand refused to answer questions about a recent probe into his organization's funding. The *Tribune* has reported that a thriving mail-order bride business underwrites the controversial group.

"Can I just explain one thing?" I asked.

"Sure."

"I need your help to clarify something about H_2O. Drixa doesn't own the patent."

"You signed it over to Aqua."

"Yes, but."

"Aqua's in charge now."

"Yes, but.

"What are you saying?"

"My signature means nothing. I signed the Letter of Agreement, but I'm not the inventor."

"Then who?"

"My maid. She's a genius."

The revelation failed to make even the slightest impression. "Ask me to tell you what to do," he said.

"What do I do?" There was a hum in the streets, or it could be on the line.

"Are you really going to listen? Pardon me for asking, but nobody listens anymore, especially you."

"Go ahead, I'm listening," I promised as the hum grew to a rumble.

"Give Drixa what they want. They're going to get it anyway, so you might as well stick with the winning team."

"ICE-9 has strategies, too. And nothing to lose."

"Who?"

"The protestors. What," I added when this got no response. "Am I barking up the wrong tree?"

"Wrong tree? Wrong forest! And you're the wrong dog. ICE-9 is a joke. Do you actually think that anyone in the Drixa boardroom ever stops to consider the demands of ICE-9? Do you think the protests have engendered a single moment of hesitation? *Gee, those kids might have a point. We really should put this stuff through a rigorous testing phase before undertaking citywide distribution.* Not happening!"

"Just be—"

"And you're not listening. I'm only going to say this once. Do whatever Drixa asks you to, except this one thing. If they say make a statement, make the statement. If they say take a dive, say okay, but—"

Although the reporter's sentence disappeared into the roar of the El train above, I still knew I heard a sharp snap. Then a burble and something like a belly-laugh, but without the laughter. The bad connection had heightened the verisimilitude of the bullet's entry. Somebody had finally taken care of Shoals. Maybe he knew this would be his last phone call, and he'd selected a fellow inside-outsider to entrust with his conclusions, someone acquainted enough with the dynamics of the organization but not ensconced in its echelons. Rather than grieving for the reporter I mourned my own prospects for the Chief Engineer job, but even this selfishness could be rationalized by explaining to myself that if they'd just given me the promotion, Shoals wouldn't have had anyone to call and might still be alive.

By getting the twice-brewing story in the *Tribune* ahead of the launch, Drixa had defused my bombshell.

Drixa wanted me alive. That was the good news. The bad news was that they only wanted me alive so I could die at the appointed time. Death by poison. Death by conspiracy. Death by public relations. "Here goes nothing," I mused, fishing for a clue.

"It will be over before you know it," Pierre said.

"That's what I'm afraid of."

The driver pulled over as we approached the Millennium Park, and Miyumi got in the back with me, but she barely acknowledged my existence. She wore tight black clothes that made her look like a lithe movie jewel thief. The crowed was smaller and less charged than anticipated. An impression came to mind, not a fear and not a daydream. I had the impression that everybody but me knew what was going on. This was the opposite of theater: the actor was the only one in the dark about the plot. It was more like a practical joke.

The protestors were busy decorating their barricades with multicolored umbrellas. Several of them wore yellow raingear. Drixa had put out some bleachers facing a semicircle of stools and a podium painted with the globular Drixa logo and the slogan: DRINK UP, IT'S DRIXA.

A plastic pitcher filled with invisible fluid almost glowed on a low table. I would be expected to drink one of three things. It might be H_2O, a synthetic product developed by Drixa to replace conventional water. It might be the latter, presented as the former because the former didn't exist. Or it might be one or the other dosed with untraceable poison or knockout drops.

Four things.

No matter how long I looked, the truth would never come out. Taste, the more reliable sense, had its own disadvantages.

"What if I don't want to do this?"

"Take all the time you want," answered Miyumi. "We're in no hurry. Pierre doesn't charge by the hour, do you, Pierre?"

"Ma'am?"

"I just told Mister Shivers you aren't charging us by the hour. You're on retainer."

"That's correct," said the driver. "But that wasn't the gentleman's question."

I tried to be stoic but didn't know what stoic felt like, so I went numb, which came close. The driver removed his gloves and announced, "As a matter of fact, it's twelve o'clock, and I'm off duty. Lovely day, think I'll take a drive."

"We can walk from here," Miyumi instructed me.

The driver continued, "Maybe you'd like to join me, Mr. Shivers."

"Me?"

"He's got other plans."

"Let's go, Hayden," Pierre Amu Lucluc encouraged. "You can sit up front with me. We'll pick up sandwiches and keep the windows open. What do you say? Roast beef and fresh air keep a man young."

Lady Miss Aqua Bella stood at the barricades, speaking into a reporter's microphone. Whatever she was saying was enthralling the reporter, who looked at her like he expected a hug.

"She's with the protestors?" I asked. "Why isn't she up on the dais?"

"This gives her a chance to reaffirm her commitment to dissenting voices."

Five or six news crews struggled into view, lugging tripods, battery packs with broken wheels, and taped-together microphone stands. The equipment was all borrowed; the cables hadn't been attached properly; the mikes were dead.

What a sad pack of grumbling chumps. An elderly technician tried to switch the portable monitor on, but his tremor made it hard to depress the button for long enough. One of the reporters was asking if anyone had a pencil he could borrow. Another requested a can of lemonade as if she were in a café and not at the launch of a history-making product. She had a high, musical laugh and wavy blond hair, and I doubted she knew the first thing about Drixa or H_2O.

The whole thing irked me. My chance to address the media had finally arrived, and the media couldn't be trusted to remove the lens cap.

The Mayor of Chicago was in the middle of his greetings. Members of the press. Our friends in the scientific community. And, significantly, he welcomed the protestors, "our guests in yellow, over there by the barricades."

"We are gathered here on March 4, a rather somber anniversary," he said. "A year ago, we were all plunged into a new world, and all we knew was that we were in this world *together*. After March 4 last year, it no longer mattered if you lived in Chicago or not, if you believed in God or not, if you spoke English or not. All that mattered was inhabiting this world together and learning to trust each other."

I couldn't quite put a finger on what he was talking about, although judging from the enrapt listeners I must have been the only one in the whole Millennium Park not getting it. Lady Miss Aqua Bella was enrapt. Miyumi was enrapt. Pierre remained parked.

You could easily lose track of the calamities that had befallen Chicago. A ferocious fire had burned for weeks in 1871. Then there were race riots, political riots, riots after sports victories and losses, killer heat waves and viruses, each of them with their own death tolls and property damages. At the end of the twentieth century, water mains used to rupture with alarming regularity. Recent years had seen the ascension of random violence, a wave of inexplicable epidemics, and innumerable crises in the infrastructure, not to mention the social wars that came with Chicago's gross and unending expansion.

What was the only explanation for these occasions when everybody else was clued in? A paranoiac would claim that people were holding secret meetings, either merely not inviting me or deliberately trying to confuse me. But I was not paranoid, I was scientific. And the scientific method led to a scientific conclusion: amnesia. Of course. Somewhere back there, a head trauma robbed me of selected events, but not enough of them that I couldn't find my way around. It could be so many things—a blow to the skull, something that I ate (or drank), an infection that had been dormant for many years. So far, I'd done a pretty good job of functioning with this condition. Unfortunately, awareness of it might corrupt my natural coping mechanism. It was like looking down and saying, Hey, I'm walking a tightrope, and then falling.

After rehashing the toll of the catastrophe in terms of human lives, dollars, and the morale of the city and the nation, the speaker asked for a moment of silence in memory of those lost, but before it could begin, he acknowledged the reporter standing by the protestors.

"Mayor King, anniversary of *what*?" came the question from one of the befuddled reporters. There was something familiar about the voice. "What happened last year on March 4?" Another case of amnesia. Must be infection. The crowd, however, seemed to murmur in assent.

"Egg-ZACT-ly!" replied the mayor. "Nothing at all happened. There was no catastrophe. Thank you, Mr. Shoals, for speaking up." My mind reeled as two theories got trounced at once.

"And do you know why there was no catastrophe? Because the Drixa Corporation averted catastrophe . . . This act goes beyond corporate citizenship and into the unprecedented realm of corporate heroism. It was an historic and inspirational moment for the modern corporation and the modern world." Everyone, including the protestors, applauded wildly. "And now it is my great pleasure to introduce the Director Emeritus of Drixa, Lionel Dawson."

Wincing into the applause, Dawson approached the podium. He seemed to look past all the people assembled before him, fixing his gaze on me. "Fresh water is the blood of our land," he began. "The nourishment of our forests and crops, the blue and shining

161

beauty at the heart of our landscape. Religions bathe their children and their saved with water. From ancient Greece, to Alaska's Koyukon Indians, to the kid down the block at her lemonade stand, one thing remains constant: where there is water, there is life. A healthy human being will die in less than a week without fresh water. A mere two percent drop in body water triggers fuzzy short-term memory, trouble with basic math, and difficulty focusing.

"Drixa has lived by the grace of water since the company was founded in 1968 as a bottled water distributor. We've moved into filtration, then desalinization, and now, synthesis, fully aware of water's importance, of its sacredness. We are here to celebrate an act of unmistakable genius and bold innovation. To communicate to you the magnitude of this accomplishment, I must ask you to combine in your minds two milestones of the past: Ben Franklin's discovery of electricity and Tom Edison's invention of the lightbulb."

I felt myself blushing, basking. The sacrifice, though invisible, demanded acknowledgment. Dawson seemed to be looking right at me.

"No one person can take credit for the genius of H_2O," the Director announced. "H_2O has destroyed many myths, and one of these is the myth of individual genius. Clever and even brilliant ideas have emerged from various constituents of our exceptional staff, but any claim of sole responsibility for H_2O would elicit shock and then laughter from the Drixa family."

I swooned inwardly, steadying myself against Miyumi's shoulder as hot blood poured into my face.

"He's great," she said, mistaking my indignation for awe. Miyumi's loyalty was as sharp as a razor. The protestors had fallen silent. The reporters muttered into phones and microcasette recorders. There was Julian leaning against a concrete planter, staring into the mouth of a plastic cup filled to the brim with water. Or something.

"I'd like to introduce a member of the Drixa family to you now. Hayden Shivers designed the drain, which, after modifications were made at the behest of the pumping squad and the corrosion task force, enabled the company to run our fountains with fifteen percent greater efficiency. I personally invited Hayden to come up here and take the ceremonial first sip of H_2O, because he represents the spirit of cooperation found at every level of Drixa culture.

"Now, unfortunately, I don't see Hayden out there right now. Hayden?" (Hand shielding eyes from nonexistent sunrays.) "He must have had a family emergency, or else I'm sure he'd have been here. But no matter, we're going to forge ahead with the ceremony, as I call upon Oliver Wright, a pipefitter in our Metrics and Retrofits Department and, of course, a member of that great bunch of guys, Pipefitters 2220, a group that went above and beyond above and beyond during the installation of this highly technical system."

Hands on my back pushed and fingers on my forearm tugged. Miyumi and Pierre were nudging me foward, urging me to declare my presence to the assembly.

"That's your signal, Hayden."

"Come on, Hayden," said Julian as I passed him. "The music's almost finished, and nearly everybody has found their seat."

I felt stunned, tranquilized, trapped. I'd grown accustomed to regarding myself as Chief Engineer and hadn't reconciled fantasy with the treason I committed by signing the patent over to Aqua Bella—who would soon be Director, but of course they knew I didn't know that at the time. Flight was redundant, fight impossible. My mouth tasted like pennies. The stool that had been set out for me was higher than the one I'd practiced with, and the seat was upholstered in vinyl, which would be less conducive to sliding.

Oliver Wright approached the dais, pumping his fist at his pipe-fitting buddies. The sleeves of his dress shirt were pushed up to reveal inappropriately dainty wrists. This was just the kind of goof that would blow the whole thing. In spite of all the money and effort poured into the spectacle, there were simply too many ways it could bomb. A misjudgment in casting, a failure to account for every possibility. The bigger a project, the greater the need for cautionary measures. But cautionary measures also increased the project's size. Drixa was cycling toward collapse.

An ambulance blinked its siren and slowly rolled away from the crowd. One of the cameramen abruptly switched off his unit and turned to go. The protestors began removing their raingear.

"Here!" I shouted. It was a strangled shout, at best. "Hayden Shivers, right here."

After a brief moment of uncertainty, the crowd opened a path for me and the protestors let out a cheer. The driver slapped me on the back and told me again to take the stage.

Ascending the dais made me lightheaded, and, thinking I had come upon Dawson, I extended a hand to Oliver Wright.

"Drink up," sneered the pipefitter, slinking away.

"It's Drixa," I agreed.

From that point on, everything progressed frame by frame, like a film traveling through a faulty projector. The rest of Dawson's speech was muffled, except for some words that came out too loud. DISASTER. THIRST. PROMISE. DROUGHT. TEST OF OUR METTLE. WAKE-UP CALL. His language made me feel small, like a sample on a slide.

This was my time to approach the stool.

The microphone was thrust into my hands, and its body-temperature handle extracted a short speech from me, the substance of which belonged to somebody else entirely. "Thank you all for coming," it began. "Especially those of you who almost stayed home, who decided at the last minute or whose other, better plans fell apart. Throughout history, and in every walk of life, the people who almost don't get there make all the difference. I myself was nearly detained by a sequence of events that barely allowed me to stand before you today.

"When I mount that stool and sip that liquid, as the liquid pours down my throat, I respectfully ask you to meditate on consumption. On co-operation. And on self-abnegation. What you are about to witness contains elements of all three, as you will undoubtedly notice."

Every one of these words surprised me as it left my throat, but collectively they galvanized the audience, whose distraction vanished. They arranged themselves in a galaxy of silent anticipation, wanting more, but I had run out of things to say. The sky had an appropriately clinical light, presenting Chicago as a mere trial city in preparation for constructing the real thing a few years from now.

Adjusting my collar, I stepped toward the pitcher of water. Pouring was difficult with one hand so I impatiently flung the microphone to the ground, producing a second or two of rolling thunder that took nobody but me by surprise. I jumped back and came very close to the edge of the dais. They put the stool too close, I fumed.

"What?" I turned to Lionel, the ex-Director, standing with hands clasped behind.

"I didn't say anything," he replied.

Up onto the stool, first one buttock then the other. The water looked clear in the pitcher but in the glass it was cloudy and garbage scented. Nausea swept over me, and then something struck me as obscenely funny. What if I fell off the stool before even taking a sip?

The surface of the liquid in the glass was slightly curved. What was the word for that?

I was born in 1980, the year that California's governor declared trees to be an oxygen-stealing national threat, but the world didn't start going to hell until I was in my mid-twenties. The litany of catastrophe was long, and amnesia—if that's what this was—was an acceptable, even necessary, defense mechanism. These memory problems had their redeeming qualities. It was possible to forget your worries little by little, year by year, and stop when you achieved a state of contented but not drooling senility, the so-called wisdom of old age, and with luck I could hope to attain it after only thirty-nine years.

I smiled, raising the glass to my lips but stopping just inches away. In my attenuated shadow, the gap yawned to the length of a pencil.

Meniscus. That was the word for that curve.

The crowd's pity and malice engulfed me. Somebody shouted something that sounded like "knife fight," and I began considering what this phrase might mean until I remembered what was expected of me. Gathering my center of gravity into my diaphragm, I concentrated, relaxed, and exhaled, letting my body spill downward, against the small table, upsetting the pitcher, and two legs of the stool cracked before my head hit the ground. The rest of me followed, piece by piece like apples from a sack. In the end I was arranged in a lopsided pyramid, which then began a slow collapse interrupted by jerks that may or may not have been involuntary. By the time I was entirely settled, the prolonged set of motions that got me there was already playing itself back in my mind, seeming delightfully slapstick—a pratfall worthy of Charlie Chan. Or, no, Charlie Chaplin. I felt my diaphragm kick with inappropriate laughter. Remaining perfectly still was almost impossible. A sharp pain in my right shin and in the bone under my right eye made the whole thing even funnier.